You're
a**ROCK**
Sister.
Lewis

You're a ROCK Sister. Lewis

SUSAN DEAN SMALLWOOD

HATRACK RIVER
PUBLICATIONS

Greensboro, North Carolina

Cover art by Paul Mann
Cover design by James Fedor and Richard Hull
This book was set in 16-point Glyphix "Oxford" and "Exchequer Script"
    from SWFTE International, using WordPerfect 5.0 and a Hewlett-
    Packard LaserJet II. It was then reduced and printed as approxi-
    mately 12-point type on acid-free paper.
Printed by Publisher's Press, Salt Lake City UT
Sole distributor of books from Hatrack River Publications is:
    Publishers Book Sales, Inc.
    805 West 1700 South
    Salt Lake City UT 84104

First printing December 1989
10 9 8 7 6 5 4 3 2 1

Library of Congress Catalog Card Number: 89-81619

ISBN 0-9624049-1-8

To Dawn —
The Melinda of my life

Other books by Susan Dean Smallwood

True Rings the Heart

Now available from Hatrack River

Kathryn H. Kidd, *Paradise Vue*

Coming from Hatrack River

Orson Scott Card, *Saints* (first hardcover edition)
Orson Scott Card, *Father, Mother, Mother, and Mom*
Kathryn H. Kidd, *Atlas Music*

Foreword
Orson Scott Card

*A*s a brand new high councilor in the Greensboro Stake, I was assigned to the Danville Ward. It was a one-hour ride north on Highway 29 to the Virginia border, and getting through Danville itself was no easy trick, especially since the directions I was following were written by someone who hadn't been to Danville in a couple of years. Roads keep shifting around in this part of the country, and folks aren't too fussy about putting up noticeable signs. I guess they figure that if you aren't from around here, you're probably up to no good, so everybody'll be better off if it takes you a mite longer to get where you're going. If you get there at all.

I got there to find the meeting already in progress. It was a small building across from a huge cemetery and dwarfed by towering trees; inside, there was room to spare for the scant attendance. Danville was a city in decline, and despite the best efforts of members and missionaries, the ward hadn't been able to add new members as fast as old ones moved away.

Still, it was a good group of people — size hasn't that much to do with spirit. I noticed right away that one of the largest families in the ward consisted of billions of children and one woman with an expression of ineffable patience. One of the children was in a wheelchair. Most of the others were in a state of constant (but quiet) motion on the hard folding chairs. It was not until one of the children broke free from the pack, charged up to the front of the room, and leapt onto the lap of one of the counselors in the bishopric that I realized this saintly woman was not actually alone in dealing with the children.

Before I left Danville that day I had become well acquainted with the Smallwood clan. Gene was a tax accountant at the time, a big gruff bear of a man who had an air of resigned humor about the difficulties of the Danville Ward — nearly thirty home teaching families per home teaching pair, for instance, and only a handful of priesthood holders to staff dozens of ward positions.

However, it was his wife, Susan, who quickly cemented our friendship. Susan, you see, was a writer. As I looked around at the herd of children browsing around her in the hall of the meetinghouse, I openly marveled that she found time to write.

"I don't *find* time," she said. "I neglect my children."

But they didn't look neglected. They looked like children who were confident of their parents' love. Happy children who were having a lot of fun being alive and didn't care how many people knew about it.

As time went by, I saw Susan in action again and again. I was in charge of the stake activities committee, and so I had the job of approving the scripts of all the wards' road shows. There were many good ones, but the script from Danville Ward was especially good. It was about a harried housewife who, in passing through the grocery store checkout line, happened to win a whole slew of hilarious, useless prizes. Funny, witty, satirical, fast-paced — and truthful enough about the life of a harried housewife that it stung, just a little bit, as good comedy always does.

Now, I've long been in the habit of refusing to look at other writers' manuscripts. It isn't that I'm not willing to give other writers a hand. I've just found that it's a completely useless thing to do. Most of the time, the writer just wants me to read his book and tell him it's so wonderful that I've sent it off to my agent to sell it for a tidy little seven-figure advance. Of course, they never *say* that this is what they want. They *say* they want me to give them advice about how to make it "good enough."

"Good enough" is a code word for "instantly marketable." What they never seem to realize is that if their book isn't already marketable, then when I give them advice on how to *make* it marketable, it will always involve *rewriting the book*. So when I sit down with them and say, "You've chosen the wrong viewpoint character and you start about six chapters too late. You need to throw away this draft and start over," they smile grimly and thank me very much and ignore everything I've said.

So I often claimed, in those days, that every writer who had ever followed my advice on a manuscript had sold it. People always ask me, "And how many is that?" To which my answer is, "None. No one ever follows my advice."

Out of a reflex born of sad experience, I had explained all this to Susan the moment she mentioned that she was a writer. Which was fine — she didn't ask me to read her novel. But after reading her road show script, I realized that this woman was the real thing. That she had the language and vision and sense of story to make a career out of writing. So, as I remember it, *I* asked *her* to let me read her book.

Susan defied all my previous experience by actually doing everything that I suggested. Her attitude was completely professional; she wasn't in love with every sentence of her writing and seemed to have no qualms about throwing out a chapter and doing it over. But the story — there she had an unerring sense of what people do, how they are with each other. Her characters were real, her dialogue was clever and entertaining, and the story involved me from the beginning to the end.

Perhaps the most important aspect of the story to me was the tale of Melinda. I knew that Melinda was modeled on Susan's sweet and beautiful daughter Dawn, who was born with cerebral palsy. At that time my wife and I were just learning to deal with our third child, newborn Charlie, who also was born with cerebral palsy (though of a different variety). The natural and easy way that Susan and Gene treated Dawn was a model to us, and their matter-of-fact attitude toward Dawn's brain damage helped calm me. I realized that Charlie was my child first, and a brain-damaged child second; and what could have been a time of desperation became one of hope and love.

So I wanted Susan's novel to succeed, not just because it was an excellent novel, but also because it could help others understand something about living with a crippling birth defect in the family.

Several years later, my wife, Kristine, and I decided that we would start an LDS publishing company of our own, in order to publish fiction that dealt frankly, sympathetically, and often comically with the lives of Saints who are committed to the Church and the gospel. The very hour that we made the decision to move ahead with Hatrack River Publications, I was on the phone with Susan Dean Smallwood.

Her second novel was not yet available for us to consider. But that was fine — what I wanted was *You're a Rock, Sister Lewis*. Was it still available? It was. Would she let me publish it? She would.

So Susan's first novel also became the first book acquired by Hatrack River for our new line of LDS fiction. Only a short while later, Susan called us with the news that another publisher was on the verge of buying her second novel. The two companies would be racing to be the first to publish a Susan Dean Smallwood novel.

We won.

You're
a ROCK
Sister.
Lewis

1

*A*llison glanced at the pile of clothes she had been folding and then out the window, where her visiting teachers were just driving up. If she worked fast she could restore the living room before they reached the door. Everyone knew, of course, that a home full of small children sometimes got cluttered, but it wasn't good to advertise the fact the way her living room was doing at this moment. Especially if your visiting teacher was also the homemaking leader.

As they got out of the car she picked up the pile of clothes and pushed them back into the clothesbasket. She slid the clothesbasket into the kitchen. As they walked up the sidewalk she shoved all the wooden blocks under the couch with her foot. As they reached the front door and rang the doorbell she opened the hall closet and threw the box of Cheerios the boys had left on the couch up on the top shelf. She made sure she shut the closet door.

"Hello, Sister McFarren. Hi, Becky," she said as she opened the front door. "Come on in."

"I hope we're not bothering you," Sister McFarren said.

"Not at all," Allison said. "I was just folding a few clothes."

"You sweet thing," Sister McFarren answered. "You just do so much."

Becky and Allison smiled at each other as Sister McFarren walked into the living room. "Folding clothes just comes with families," Allison said.

"I don't know how you keep up with it all, Allison," Becky said. "My laundry piles up with just the three of us."

"Oh, you just wait," Sister McFarren said. "A few years from now you will look back on this time of folding all those clothes for all these sweet little children and remember them as the best times of your life."

"I'm sure I will, Sister McFarren," Allison said. "Please sit down." She motioned to a chair, then hurried to pick up the pair of tennis shoes she'd overlooked in the chair.

"Where are all your children?" Becky asked. "Your house seems awfully quiet." Becky talked to Allison on the phone enough to know that her house was not often so quiet.

Allison counted them off on her fingers. "Sharon and Andrew don't get home until three-thirty. Melinda's minibus gets here in about thirty minutes. And the little boys are asleep."

She changed her mind as two crashes punctuated her sentence. "Then again, maybe they are awake now." She listened for a cry of pain but none came.

"What was that?" Sister McFarren asked.

"As we say around here," Allison said. "The Disastrous Duo strikes again. Let me go see what they've done now." She could hear giggling as she walked down the hall so she knew they weren't dead.

Mark was four and Matthew was barely three. One week Mark was the hurricane and Matthew was the tornado. The next week they switched.

Allison groaned softly as she opened the door to their bedroom. Mark was standing near a pile of what seemed to be every piece of clothing they owned. The crashes had been their dresser drawers falling on the floor. Their dresser was now filled with what seemed to be every toy they owned. And Matthew was nowhere to be seen.

"Hi, Mommy," Mark said. "We're reorganizing our drawers."

She hated to but she had to smile at his big words. Somehow he always seemed to use them at his (or was it her?) most desperate moments.

Just then she heard a giggle and the toys piled in the dresser began to wiggle. A brown head with big brown eyes popped out. "Peek-a-boo," Matthew said.

Allison pulled him out of the dresser, a dozen toys falling around him. She put him on the bed then picked Mark up and plopped him beside Matthew. Shaking her finger, she looked down at them as sternly as she could. "Look at this mess you have made for us to pick up." Then she dropped her voice to a whisper. "If you'll stay on the bed while Mommy's company is here and play quietly I'll give you cookies after they leave. And I'll make Kool-aid."

It was an offer no child could refuse.

"Okay, Mommy," Mark said.

"'Kay, Mommy," Matthew echoed.

Suddenly Sister McFarren was at the bedroom door. "Anything your visiting teachers can help with?"

"Oh no," Becky said behind her as she caught sight of the room.

Allison smiled apologetically. "They were trying to clean up."

"Guess what?" Mark said from the bed. "Mommy's going to give us cookies and Kool-Aid if we shut up until you go home."

Allison laughed weakly. "I didn't say it that way."

"Aren't they sweet?" Sister McFarren said.

Allison had to admit they looked cute cuddled up together. Brown curls, big brown eyes, and a scattering of freckles. Who could stay angry at them for long?

Then she looked back at the mess that Sister McFarren and Becky were attempting to straighten up and knew that she could manage a few minutes more. "Mark, you are in charge. I want you to pick up all your toys and put them back in the toy box, then put your clothes back in the drawers. I'll straighten them out later."

"And then it's cookie time?" Mark asked.

"And then it's cookie time," she promised. She took some clothes from Sister McFarren. "They can do it, Sister McFarren. Let's go back in the living room."

When they sat down again Sister McFarren pulled out the visiting teaching message. "It's on being a good example," she said.

"You don't need to read it," Becky said. "You're already a good example."

"Me?" Allison said. She had been right in picking up the living room before they came.

"You," Becky said. She handed the message over.

As Allison reached for it she saw that Melinda's minibus had pulled up and her driver was lowering her wheelchair down on the lift.

"Excuse me a minute," Allison said. "I need to get Melinda in."

"We need to leave anyway," Becky said. They both stood up and followed Allison out onto the porch.

Sister McFarren watched as Melinda's driver pushed her wheelchair up the sidewalk. She turned to Allison and squeezed her arm. "You dear sister," she said. "I just don't see how you do what you do."

"I sure couldn't do it," Becky said.

"Oh yes, you could," Allison said.

"You are a rock," Sister McFarren said. "A real rock."

Allison didn't quite know how to answer such a compliment, if indeed it was one, so she just thanked them for coming and walked down to meet Melinda.

She smiled as she always did when she got to her. Melinda was beautiful and if she hadn't been sitting in the wheelchair it would be hard to know that she needed one. She had the same brown curls her little brothers had but hers were pulled back with a pretty ribbon. Her big brown eyes sparkled in between their long thick lashes and a few freckles skipped across her nose.

The thing that most people noticed about Melinda first, though, was the beautiful smile that lit up her face. A doctor had told Allison once that a big smile was a characteristic of the type of brain-injury that Melinda had but Allison felt it was more the characteristic of the sweet and laughing little girl whose spirit escaped the bonds her body placed upon her.

Today she was wearing a big construction paper badge that stated in magic marker "Super Girl." She beamed as her driver pushed her up to Allison and said, "Melinda's teacher said to tell you that she did a great job today in school. She worked real hard on her reading and knew all of her words."

"That's great, Melinda," Allison said. She bent down and gave her a kiss. "I'm real proud of you." She took over the steering of the wheelchair as her driver walked away. "Tell him good-bye, Melinda."

"Bye-bye," Melinda said with difficulty and a great deal of concentration.

Allison was thrilled to hear just those two words. Until last year no one had been able to understand much that she tried to say. But with speech therapy and many hours of work in the evenings at home her speech had improved to such a point that she could say sentences of several words with enough clarity that she could be understood.

As she pushed Melinda up the ramp to the porch her thoughts shifted from Melinda's speech to the comment that Sister McFarren had made. If she had a dollar for every time the last six years that someone had said to her "I don't see how you do what you — I couldn't do it" she really believed that she could buy the electric wheelchair that Melinda's therapists had recommended.

Sometimes when people said that, she felt complimented that they thought she could manage her busy life and large family well. Other times, though, she could just cry when they said it, because she certainly hadn't asked to have a handicapped child, at least not in this life, and sometimes she didn't manage well at all. She cried and just wished that someone else would try to handle all this and give her a break.

Stop feeling sorry for yourself, Allison, she thought as she parked Melinda in the living room. Lots of people have problems. Everyone does. That's the purpose of life. She didn't really want to be problem-free, anyway — she'd just like to change problems every few years. But even as she wished that, she knew deep down that the problem in her life that caused her heart to break every time she looked at Melinda struggle with an unwilling body would be around for an awfully long time.

A strangling sound from the kitchen interrupted her thoughts. She set the brake on Melinda's wheelchair to go investigate but before she could get there Matthew and Mark appeared at the living room door. Matthew was the one strangling as red stains dripped from his mouth. Mark was pounding him on the back. "Save him, Mommy. Save him," he shouted.

"What's wrong?" She rushed over to him and took over the pounding. "Where's he bleeding from?"

"It's not bleed," Mark said. "It's Kool-Aid. We were trying to help you make our surprise and he wanted to eat the Kool-Aid without the water. I don't think he likes it."

After a glass of water stopped the strangling, Allison sat him on the kitchen counter to check for broken ribs. She turned to Mark. "Could you very, very carefully push Melinda through the kitchen door while I make the Kool-Aid? And please don't ever try to make it by yourselves again unless you ask Mommy first."

As she wiped up the counter and took deep breaths to stop her heart from thumping she reviewed the emergency number as she always did with false alarms. Then she calmly said, "By the way, Mark. It isn't *bleed*. It's *blood*."

Mark looked at her, shaking his head. "Silly Mommy," he said. "It isn't blood. It's *Kool-Aid*."

2

A couple of hours later Allison had shifted into her afternoon routine. Everyone was home from school and she felt in control of her family again. She could stop worrying about kidnappings and bad influences and struggle with getting Andrew to set the table and Sharon to get off the phone.

She stood at the sink peeling carrots and dodging the little cars Mark and Matthew were speeding across the kitchen floor. They had assured her that they weren't trying to get as close to her feet as possible but she wondered. Andrew was working on his homework in his room as diligently as ever. Sharon was sitting in the family room with Melinda on her lap watching Sesame Street. Allison made a mental note to tell her once more how much she appreciated her help with Melinda.

Any minute now Brian would walk through the front door, set his briefcase down in the hall closet, and walk into the kitchen to place a kiss on the back of her neck. She was pondering the effect on the male ego of having your wife's neck in the same place at the same time every day and whether Phil Donahue would approve, when she heard him come through the door. She heard the closet door open and the briefcase hit the floor. She waited for the kiss. When it didn't come she turned around and saw him standing at the kitchen door brushing something out of his hair.

"Who booby-trapped the closet?" he asked. "I opened the door and a box of Cheerios fell all over me."

"Oh, I'm sorry," she said. She helped him brush; it was the least she could do. "My visiting teachers came and I sort of threw the Cheerios up there to save my reputation."

"You have a reputation?" Brian asked. "Maybe you'd better tell me about it."

"You know Sister McFarren," Allison said. "She thinks I'm wonderful."

"You are," he said. He grabbed her around the waist and gave her a hug.

"Not *wonderful* wonderful. More like capable." She returned his hug. "She thinks I breeze through my life loving every minute of this and counting my many blessings as I go. She told me today I was a rock."

"Was that a compliment?"

"You tell me."

Just then the boys, realizing their Daddy was home, came running and grabbed him around the knees. "Hi, Daddy," they shouted in unison.

Brian groaned as the force of impact hit. "Hi, boys," he said. "Be careful with Daddy. His back has been killing him today." He patted them on their heads. "Go eat the Cheerios off the floor in the hall."

"All right," Mark yelled and headed down the hall.

"Right, Daddy," Matthew echoed and followed.

Allison turned back from the sink where she had returned to the carrots. "Is your back worse, honey?" He had had back trouble for the last couple of years but never serious enough — so he said — to go see a doctor.

"I think splitting the wood last night hurt my back more than usual."

"Here, sit down a minute and rest while I finish getting supper ready." Allison pulled a placemat over and patted the table, but Brian just stood there looking a little uncomfortable.

"Actually," he said. "I thought maybe, if it's okay with you, that I would go lie down for a little bit — like maybe the rest of the night. It really hurts to sit down." He waited expectantly.

For a split second Allison blanched. He looked so uncomfortable and humble that she couldn't refuse him for long even though he was so good about helping with supper and baths that she preferred not being without him. His job as a CPA meant late hours during tax season but this was September and she'd had him home for several months. But when she took into account her love for him and his obvious pain as he stood before her, bent slightly, holding onto the back of the chair, what was a loving wife to do?

So she kissed him on the cheek and picked another Cheerio crumb out of his mustache. "You go lie down right now and don't even think about getting up until tomorrow. I'll bring your supper in to you as soon as it's ready," she said. "Do you need any help?"

"No, I think I can handle it." He walked out but added over his shoulder, "Call if you need me."

Of course, she always needed him, but even knowing he was in the house gave her a happy feeling as she faced supper, the hour of the day designed to test her real commitment to the high ideals of motherhood. Dinnertime was what all Mother's Day talks were really about. All that talk of sacrifice and patience.

But tonight dinner was almost peaceful. Sharon played the airplane games to persuade Melinda to eat while Andrew helped wipe her mouth and jumped up to get all the things that had been left off the table. Allison sat between the two little boys as they quickly ate their dinner and ran off to watch TV in bed with their Daddy. Allison was indulging in a second helping of mashed potatoes when the phone rang. It was Bishop Murphy.

"Hi, Allison," he said. "How are you tonight?"

"Just fine," she said. "How are you?"

"Pretty good, except that my first counselor and I are sitting over here at the church wondering if our second counselor had forgotten the bishopric meeting tonight."

"Oh, he must have," she said. "He came home with his back hurting and went right in to lie down."

"Is that back still hurting him?" the bishop asked. "Maybe he needs to go see a doctor." He hesitated a minute. "Could I ask you something and you tell me whether or not it's okay. I mean really all right. Oh, never mind."

"What?" she said. "Tell me what you need."

"Well, do you think that maybe we could come over for just a few minutes and meet with him? Not too long — just a little while, an hour at the most, to iron out some of the budget problems. We won't stay long. In fact, we won't come at all. It was a stupid idea."

"No, no," she said. "I'll go ask him. Hang on."

She walked back to the bedroom. "Brian, did you forget the bishopric meeting?" She thought she heard a muffled "Oh, no" but she wasn't sure because his head was under a pillow. "Matthew! Mark! Don't suffocate your father. Get off of his head."

"We're giving him swimming lessons," Mark said.

Allison pulled the boys off the pillow and Brian pulled the pillow off his head. "I'm learning to hold my breath. I've made it to a minute." He smiled. "What's this about a bishopric meeting? The bishop remembered something I forgot?"

"Evidently," she said. "He wants to know if they can come over for a few minutes. Something about the budget."

He put the pillow over his head as he groaned. "Sure, tell them to come over. They can gather around my sickbed." His voice disappeared under the pillow again as the boys jumped back on him. As she walked down the hall she heard Matthew say, "Let's try for five minutes, Daddy."

She made it through the evening and the evening's responsibilities without Brian and had to admit she'd done a pretty good job. She had even found time to work on Melinda's speech homework, holding up pictures and having Melinda describe them with three words. School clothes had been laid out and the living room straightened up for at least the tenth time since her visiting teachers had visiting taught. Or was it visit teached? She could never remember how you actually said what they did after they'd done it.

The bishop and Brother Moore had been gone quite a while when Allison decided to give up on the letter she was writing and get some sleep. Brian was lying in bed reading the newspaper when she climbed in.

"Good-night," she said. Then, "How was your meeting? Did you get the budget straightened out?"

"Not yet," he said. "My mind seems to know when my body has a suit on and when it has pajamas on and works accordingly. Besides, my back was hurting so much that I couldn't really concentrate too well."

"Maybe you should go see a doctor, Brian. It's been hurting for a long time — maybe it's something serious."

"Do you know how much that would cost?" It was a popular question with him.

"All you accountants ever think about is the cost of things," she answered. That was a popular response with her. She kissed him and turned over. "Well, good-night," she said. "I'm tired."

He didn't respond and she was just about to drop off to sleep when he said in a funny sort of voice, "Allison?"

She managed a "Huh?"

"Can I ask you something?"

"I guess so."

"Would you accept the calling as Young Women President?"

"You're kidding," she said. "Plus you're crazy."

"Is that a no?"

Most of the time Allison loved his sense of humor. It gave her a sense of balance in her life. Tonight she was too tired, though, to listen to the ramblings of a man in too much pain to think clearly. And she told him that.

"I'm sorry, honey, but I'm serious," he said. "Sister Spence is needed somewhere else and she suggested your name to replace her as Young Women President. I told the bishop I would ask you about it."

He had her full attention now. "Honey, I can't do that." She sat straight up in bed and looked disparagingly at him. "I can't even handle what I have to do now."

"Oh, Allison. You do a great job with the kids, especially Melinda."

"I do not," she said.

"You do, too," he said again.

"I do not. And don't disagree with me. Go look in the refrigerator."

"Why?"

"It needs cleaning out. So do all the closets. And you know I never can get all the laundry done at the same time." She sat back, satisfied that she had proven herself incompetent and unable to accept the calling.

"So what?" he said. "It's not easy to take care of a large family and a handicapped child as well as you do." He looked at her seriously, more like a member of the bishopric than a husband. "You think and pray about it and let me know. You know I'd help you all I can. I know you'd do a great job."

She sank back onto the bed. "I would not," she muttered and buried her head in her pillow. "They wouldn't do this to me out in Utah."

Brian laughed. "Out in Utah they have enough people to fill all the callings in a ward. They probably have sisters who would beg for this calling."

"I wouldn't fight them for it," she said.

Brian patted her on the back. "You are a rock, Sister Lewis. After you get a good night's sleep everything will look better."

She closed her eyes but she didn't feel like a rock. And her good night's sleep had just been ruined.

3

*A*llison heard the clock radio come on and wiggled just enough to acknowledge that she was awake. Her thoughts drifted until she heard the song that was playing. It was a song that was popular when she and Brian were first married and she never heard it without thinking about being newly-married and poor at BYU.

She turned over to shake Brian. "Honey, do you hear that song? Do you remember it playing in the mornings when we were getting ready to go to classes at the Y?"

"Mmmm," he said. Brian was not a morning person.

"And remember the commercial that would come on about the Tuesday spaghetti dinner special at Heap's and we could never even afford that?"

"Mmmm," he said.

Allison dug around under the pillow until she found his hand to hold. She lay back on her pillow, basking in the memories of their earlier days when Sunday mornings were unrushed and she had only herself to get ready for church.

And she lived in a ward large enough to overlook over-worked people like her.

Then she remembered. Today was the Sunday morning she had to face the bishop to give him her deci-sion. She had spent the last two days wondering and worrying about what she was going to say to him. She knew what she wanted to say to him, but she had never turned down a church calling before. But then she had never been asked to lead, guide, and walk beside a group (or was it a mob?) of teenage girls before. She hadn't even liked teenagers much when she was one.

She untangled her fingers from Brian's and started gently, but seriously, shaking him awake. "Brian, Brian," she said. "What am I going to do about Young Women's?"

"Haven't you made your decision yet?" he mumbled.

"No," she said. She got out of bed. "I'm hoping when I get to church that a new family will have moved in the ward with six teenage daughters and a gung-ho mother and the bishop will forget he ever knew me."

She shook him again, more seriously than gently this time. "Come on and help me get all these children ready for church."

As she walked into the bathroom she heard the radio announcer say, with a chuckle, that her wonderful song was a "golden oldie." That made it official; her mood had changed. The romantic feeling was gone. She was now capable of facing Sunday morning with her children.

"Sunday morning at the Lewis home and look what Mommy has for breakfast," Allison announced grandly. She took a large pan from the oven and put it in the middle of the table with a flourish.

"Cinnamon rolls!" Mark shouted. He and Matthew started jumping up and down on the bench clapping their hands.

"Not only cinnamon, but apple and cheese-filled," she said. "Sit down, boys, and I'll give you one."

"But, Mom, they're fattening," Sharon said.

"Not if this is all you have to eat," Allison said. "And this is it, troops. We are simplifying our Sunday mornings." She sat down and handed out napkins. Then she pushed Melinda's wheelchair over so she could feed her.

"Did I hear someone say cinnamon rolls?" Brian asked. He walked into the kitchen with his briefcase. He had an early bishopric meeting. "Did you make them?"

"Almost," Allison said. "I put the finishing touches on them — heating them up." She spooned some oatmeal into Melinda's mouth and tore off a little piece of cinnamon roll to tempt her.

"She says she's simplifying our Sundays," Sharon said. "But she's going to make me fat."

"You're too skinny," Brian said. "You could use some fattening up." He looked at his daughter then added, "You could also take some of that red stuff off your cheeks."

"It's called blush," she said. "And I don't have too much on, do I, Mom?"

"Maybe a little," Allison said. She reached over and wiped off a little with a napkin. "There."

"Sharon wants to look pretty for the boys," Andrew said.

Sharon blushed. "I do not."

"Don't tease your sister," Brian said. Reaching across the table, he patted Allison on the head. It was the best he could do with all the little bodies between them. "I'll see you later, honey. Are you going with me, son?" he asked Andrew. Andrew liked to go early and have some peace and quiet on Sunday mornings.

"Sure, Dad," Andrew said. "I need to practice my part for the sacrament meeting program next week." He picked up the scriptures he had gotten for baptism and they left.

Sacrament meeting program. Allison had forgotten all about that. She spooned more oatmeal into Melinda's mouth, scraped off what she lost, and tried to remember where she had put the little boys' parts.

"Mom," Sharon said with exasperation. "Look what Matthew did. He wiped his sticky mouth all over my blouse.

Now I've got to go change." She wiped at her blouse with a napkin while she held Matthew at arm's length.

"Here's his lapkin," Mark said. He picked it off the bench and, holding Matthew at the back of his neck, began wiping the frosting off his mouth with the napkin.

"Owie, owie," Matthew cried.

"Here, honey, I'll do it," Allison said. "Let's let him keep his lips." She wiped a little more gently. "Sharon, go get a wet washcloth. I think that will take the frosting off your blouse."

"Okay, Mom," she answered. She groaned as she got up from the table. "Mom, they're licking all the frosting off. That's so disgusting." She started out of the kitchen shaking her head, but turned before she left and said, "I'll read some stories to Melinda while you get ready if you want."

"Can we read, too? Can we?" Mark asked. "I want the one where the wolf gets his head chopped off."

Sharon sighed reluctantly. "Only if you won't do anything to stain me."

"Yippee, yippee," Mark shouted with Matthew joining in. Then they started karate-chopping each other on the neck in anticipation.

"Thanks, sweetie," Allison said. She looked at the clock and started shoveling oatmeal faster.

They made it to church on time — Allison hoped that meant it was her lucky day. She unbuckled Matthew and Mark, letting them loose with orders to go find their Daddy inside. Then she unlocked the trunk, pulled out the wheelchair, and reassembled it. She unbuckled and unpillowed Melinda from her seat in the car and with a mighty heave-ho lifted her from her place in the back seat and gently plopped her in the wheelchair. All done.

It was at this point that someone usually came out and asked if they could help her with anything. But no one was in the parking lot today and she didn't see anyone until she reached the door where Brother Wingate held the heavy doors open for her.

"Good morning, Sister Lewis," he said, holding out his hand. She rearranged the books and diaper bag dangling from her one arm that was not pushing the wheelchair, put her foot up on the wheelchair to keep it from rolling, and shook his hand. Brother Wingate was a very patient man. He made her go through this every Sunday.

He reached his hand down to where Melinda could reach it and clutched her hand, shaking it gently up and down. As always, Allison forgave him on the spot for her handshake for Melinda loved this ritual every Sunday and rewarded him with a big smile. "Hi," she said softly.

Just then a cold chill clutched Allison's heart as she saw the bishop. He was talking to someone, though, so maybe she could avoid him for a while. She pushed Melinda quickly into the chapel and to the end of the row where they always sat as it afforded easy access to the foyer.

Where did her boys go and who could she get to watch Melinda while she went and looked for them? Ashley Moore and Jared Turner were sitting in front of her but, as usual, they were too involved with each other to know what was happening in the world beyond them. Terri Lynn Parker and her best friend Rhonda Rhodes were sitting a couple of pews over and were giggling in what they probably thought was a reverent whisper as they wrote notes on the back of the program.

Someone should teach them some reverence, she decided. Then she caught herself. I didn't mean it, she said silently. She had seen it happen before — the minute you saw a problem in the ward you were called to solve it. She wouldn't dare ask them to watch Melinda because as soon as she did the bishop would walk in, see her talking to them, and decide they needed Allison in their lives.

She felt hands on her shoulders. "Hello, Sister Lewis," Sister McFarren said. "How are you this beautiful Sabbath day? Isn't it wonderful to have a break in the week to come and meet with our brothers and sisters in the gospel?" She picked up Melinda's hand and patted it. "And don't you look just like a little angel?"

"Sister McFarren, did you happen to see my two little boys anywhere?" Allison asked.

"Yes, Sister Lewis, I did," she answered. "They were with their Daddy in the hall. He had each sweet little boy by the hand. They just love their Daddy, don't they?"

Allison's guess was that they were doing some unique experiment in the restroom or hiding all the little children in the nursery's toy box when he had caught them. Or maybe they had come up with something new.

But she just smiled at Sister McFarren and said, "Thank you. I guess he'll bring them to me before church begins."

She was sure about that. Brian considered sitting up on the stand with the bishopric one of his choicest blessings. It wasn't the prestige — it was the total lack of any of the children up there with him. He told her that it increased his love and appreciation for her as the mother of his children to watch her struggle so patiently with them every Sunday, but she told him she could do with less appreciation and more help. So he let her take a nap every Sunday afternoon while he watched the children and that evened things up. Or close enough.

Sister McFarren moved on down the aisle and Allison pushed the wheelchair as close to the pew as possible and sank down, trying to look invisible.

Even as she tried she knew it was impossible. Everyone, including the bishop, would see her when she went out of church. She couldn't even remember the last time that she had sat through a whole church meeting. If it wasn't the Disastrous Duo — although she had to admit they were improving — it was Melinda. For some reason that no one had been able to figure out, she always screamed during the sacrament hymn. She was happy until that point, looking around and smiling at everyone and even raising her arm up as far as she could when there was any sustaining or releasing to be done. But as soon as the first strains of the sacrament hymn began her lip dropped and big tears filled her eyes. Then she would scream at the top of her lungs and out Allison and Melinda would go.

The school psychologist said that it was a "learned reaction to a particular stimulus" and that she needed to be "desensitized." Sister McFarren said that she had a special spirit that was more sensitive to spiritual things than everyone else. Mark said that she cried because the sacrament hymns were always sad-sounding. Allison tended to agree with Mark but she kept hoping anyway.

This Sunday was no different and the first strains of the sacrament hymn found Allison pushing Melinda out the chapel doors. Mark had stayed wedged between Sharon and Andrew coloring Sesame Street pictures but Matthew clumped out behind her. He loved his Sunday shoes with the hard soles.

"Ow, honey," Allison said as he stepped on her foot when they stopped in front of the foyer couch. "Here, sit up here and eat some raisins." She put him up on the couch and dug around in the diaper bag until she found the raisins to give him. Melinda had already stopped crying.

"Melinda," Allison said to the little girl now smiling before her. "When are you going to stop crying during the sacrament hymns? Mommy is supposed to take the sacrament every Sunday. That was a naughty girl. What am I going to do with you?"

Melinda's response was to wave her arm toward the raisins Matthew was eating and say, "Want some." The "t" wasn't very clear and the words slurred a little but Allison knew what she meant.

"If I give you these raisins will you promise to be good in church next Sunday and not cry?" Allison asked, knowing while she said it that the psychologist would say she was rewarding negative behavior.

Melinda nodded her head as Allison put a raisin in her mouth. "Now chew carefully," she said. She leaned back on the couch, surveying the foyer. It was empty except for them. Why did everyone else have reverent children?

As she contemplated her failure as a mother and carefully placed one raisin at a time in Melinda's mouth, the chapel doors opened and two of the Young Women came giggling into the foyer.

They're everywhere today, Allison thought. I can't get away from them.

One was Terri Lynn Parker and the other was Rhonda Rhodes. Allison had trouble remembering which was which since they always came in a pair. About the only contact Allison ever had with them was through Sharon, who always wanted to go out and buy whatever they were wearing.

As they giggled their way over to the water fountain, she certainly hoped Sharon wouldn't want what they were wearing today. She wouldn't have let her daughter out of the house to go to church with all the layers of baggy sweaters they had on. And their heels were so high it was a wonder they had even made it out of the chapel without spraining something.

Just then Matthew spilled his raisins over the side of the couch and across the carpet. It was amazing that one little box could hold enough raisins to carpet a large room.

"Oh, Matthew," Allison said. "Look what a mess you've made." She slid off the couch, knelt down, and began picking up the sticky raisins before he could mash them into the carpet.

"We'll help, Sister Lewis," a voice said, and either Rhonda or Terri Lynn knelt down beside her.

Allison looked up but couldn't believe what she saw. She was looking right at whoever's ear it was and it had four earrings in it — one dangly one and three little ones all curving around the same earlobe. She glanced over at the other girl who was reaching under the couch for raisins and saw the same number of earrings in her ears. Eight pairs of earrings between two girls. Sharon better not say a thing.

"Here, Terri Lynn," said the one who was reaching under the couch. She handed over a wad of raisins.

"Thanks," Allison said, taking the raisins from the one she now knew to be Terri Lynn. "I appreciate it." She pulled out one of Melinda's mouth diapers and started wiping Matthew's sticky fingers.

"He's so cute," Rhonda said.

"Thanks," Allison said again. She wished she could think of something else to say to two girls with sixteen earrings who were obviously trying to be civilized anyway.

Suddenly they both knelt down in front of Melinda's wheelchair. Rhonda held both of Melinda's hands and Terri Lynn picked up the diaper and wiped Melinda's mouth.

"Hi, Melinda," Rhonda said. "Do you like to play patty-cake?" She patted her hands together softly. "Patty-cake, patty-cake." Melinda laughed.

"You have on such a pretty dress today, Melinda," Terri Lynn said. She smoothed out the front of it. "See the pretty flowers." She held out the hem of her dress so Melinda could see the border.

Terri Lynn stood up and said, "We'd better get back in or my mother will have a fit."

"Mine, too," Rhonda said. She stood up and, still holding Melinda's hand, waved it for her. "Bye-bye."

Then they were gone, with only Melinda's happy smile to show they had ever been there.

Allison was touched that those two girls with so many holes in their ears would know, and care, that even little girls in wheelchairs loved pretty dresses. She smiled back at Melinda.

Then suddenly she was very depressed. She wondered if you could get a sign from heaven without even wanting one. Brian would know.

It seemed forever until the meeting was over and Brian came out of the chapel. "Honey," she said as he came up to her. "I need to ask you something."

"Can it wait until we get home?" he asked. He was smiling very weakly. "I had orders to send you in to the bishop as soon as sacrament meeting was over."

"Oh, no," she whined. She hated it when she whined. Brian probably didn't love it either.

Brian faced her and put both of his hands on her shoulders. She felt the weight of the responsibility already. She looked up hopefully, hungry for inspiration and courage.

"Allison," he said. "Don't think of them as the Young Women. Think of them as potential babysitters."

"Brian!"

"Here," he said, taking over Melinda's wheelchair. "I'll take the children to Primary and you talk to the bishop."

"What am I going to say to him?" she asked desperately.

"Ask him how his squash is doing," Brian said.

"No," she said. "He might give us four more bushels." The bishop had enthusiastically reminded everyone last spring of the prophet's counsel to plant a garden and, to have an example, had planted over two hundred squash plants himself. To his surprise, they had all survived and thrived, and the whole ward had at least a two year's supply of squash in their freezer and pantry.

"You're right," Brian said. "Don't mention squash,." He thought a minute. "Tell him you need a sign — just this once," he joked.

She grabbed his arm. "Why did you say that?" she demanded.

"I was just kidding." Then he turned to the children. "Let's go to Primary, children, before your mother falls apart before our eyes."

She felt like a stupor of thought as she walked down the hall and knocked on the bishop's door.

"Sister Lewis, come in, come in," Bishop Murphy said. He motioned for her to take the chair opposite him.

She sat down and was reminded of the times she had sat in his English Lit classes in high school and prayed that he wouldn't discover she hadn't read her assignment.

He was shuffling some papers around, looking for something. "Here they are," he said, finding his glasses in his pocket and putting them on. He looked over at her puzzled. "Let's see, Sister Lewis," he said. "What did we have in mind for you today?"

I'll never tell, she thought. She smiled back at him, looking as innocent as she could.

"Ah, yes," he said. He folded his hands on the desk and leaned forward. "Sister Lewis, let me begin by saying that the gospel is a gospel of change." He thought a minute. "No, I don't mean a gospel of change actually. The gospel never changes; the church does." He hesitated again. "I don't mean changes as in basic changes. I mean that changes have to be made sometimes. Basically."

Allison waited, hoping for a whirlwind to come and whisk her away before he got too far. She hadn't wanted to be translated without Brian but at this point she'd take anything.

"Anyway, what I really want to say is that we have to make some changes in the Young Women Presidency and we want you to be it." He smiled at her then frowned slightly. "Of course, we don't want you to be the whole Young Women Presidency, just the President. You can have two counselors to help you."

"But, Bishop Murphy, I don't know if I can do that or not," she began.

"Of course you can," he said. "Everyone can have two counselors."

"I mean be the Young Women President," she said. "I don't know if I could handle all that responsibility."

"It is a lot of responsibility," he said.

"I mean — I know I could handle the responsibility because I'm a very responsible person. I'm just sort of tied down with taking care of Melinda right now."

"I'm sure that's a tremendous responsibility, Sister Lewis," he said. "And I admire the way you take such good care of her."

"You know I can't just leave her with any babysitter," Allison explained. "She could always have a seizure or choke, and she can't run away from anything dangerous like the other children."

"I had never considered that before," the bishop said. "That must be a problem. Is Brian able to watch her sometimes so you can get out?"

"Brian's real good about helping me," she said. Then she decided to add, "But during tax season he's really busy at work so I'm not sure he could always be home to babysit while I was at church."

"I can see where that might be a problem." He nodded his head slowly in understanding. "He does have to make a living."

He sat quietly, looking at her intently. She looked back at him and felt very torn inside. Church and family were supposed to all fit together nicely in her life. Why did she feel so torn between the two?

"Well, Sister Lewis," he finally said. "You've brought up a lot of points that I had not considered. But I do know that when I prayed about this particular calling I was very impressed to extend the call to you."

"You were?" she asked. She had hoped that inspiration hadn't been involved.

"I was," he said, more definitely than he said most things. "But since this is also a gospel of free agency, why don't you go home and pray and ponder about it? I'll go home and do the same and we'll talk again."

He was right. It was a gospel of free agency and she had always used hers to accept church callings. She thought of spilled raisins and of raising her hand to sustain the man being so kind to her now. Why waste her time and his time praying when she already knew what her answer would be if she prayed sincerely this time?

"That won't be necessary, bishop," she said, in a miserable tone of voice. "I'll accept the calling."

"You will?" he said.

"I will."

"Are you sure?" he said. He took his glasses off and gazed at her, puzzled again.

"I'm sure I don't want to do it," she said. "But I'm sure I'm supposed to." Her home would probably fall to pieces, her children be neglected, her marriage fail, but for some reason she knew she had to say yes.

"That's the attitude I like to hear, Sister Lewis." Now he had a big smile on his face. "I appreciate your willingness to serve."

"Well, thank you," she said. She didn't feel like she deserved the thanks. Her spirit and flesh both felt unwilling.

As she stood up to leave, the bishop disappeared behind his desk. When he sat back up he was holding a jar with little yellow chunks floating around it. It looked like he was going to give it to her, but she hoped not.

"Just to show you how much I appreciate your help in this ward, I want to give you some of the pickled squash the wife and I made."

"Oh," she said. "Thank you. I don't think we've ever had pickled squash before. It will be a really new experience."

"I hope you enjoy it," he said. "Plenty more where that came from." He held the door open for her. "Now once you're sustained next week you can get with Sister Spence and find out which night the Young Women have their activities. I can never remember."

She couldn't understand why but she had a good feeling as she walked out into the hallway. She hadn't expected to walk out of that door the Young Women President, but so far, except for the pickled squash, she didn't regret it. Of course, it had only been five minutes. There was plenty of time for regret to come later.

4

*E*verybody else's family was neatly divided up into classes. Allison's entire family, though, was waiting for her down the hall and around the corner from the bishop's office. Brian was holding Matthew who was holding his finger wrapped up in a wet paper towel. He started sobbing when he saw her. Brian was also pushing Melinda back and forth in her wheelchair as she sobbed. Sharon was holding onto Mark whose shirt was sopping wet. Andrew was standing quietly, reading his copy of the sacrament program.

"What has happened here?" Allison said. "When I saw you last you had everything under control." Mark broke loose from Sharon and ran to her.

"I was a nurse," he said. "Matthew smashed his Mister Pointer and I fixed it."

Allison took Matthew in her arms and kissed his finger. "Poor baby." She laid his head on her shoulder and turned back to Brian. "What's wrong with Melinda?"

"Beats me," he said. "I was sitting by her in Primary and she started screaming."

"What were they singing?" she asked, knowing what he would answer.

"Jesus Wants Me for A Sunbeam."

"And the Sunbeam class was wearing the yellow Sunbeam hats?"

"Yes," he said. "And she started crying so I thought she wanted one and I sent Mark up to get one. But when I put it on her she got hysterical."

Allison had been right. "She is terrified of the Sunbeam hats, honey." She bent down and patted Melinda on her arm. "It's okay, Melinda. Daddy didn't know."

"I'm sorry," Brian said.

She patted him reassuringly on the arm. "So what happened to Matthew?"

"Well," Brian said unhappily, "he had to go to the bathroom when Melinda was screaming so I sent Mark to the bathroom with him to help him."

Mark took over the explanation. "And he got his finger smashed in the door so I put some water on a paper towel like you do and wrapped it up." He stuck up his finger and demonstrated the bandaging technique. "I was a great doctor. Except I got a little wet." He held the front of his shirt out and it dripped on the floor.

"That was real smart of you to take care of your brother like that," Allison said. She patted him on the head as she turned to Andrew. "So what's your problem, Andrew?"

"Oh, I don't have a problem, Mom," he said. "I came to tell you that Sister Benson wants to talk to you."

"What's wrong?" she asked. Sister Benson was the Primary President. After what had just happened with her family in Primary she was probably going to request they attend another ward.

Brian groaned and shook his head. "That's just what we need in our life — more excitement."

"Mother," Sharon said just then. "Please tell me I can go back to class and leave this crazy family."

"Sure," Allison said. "Just remember you have to come home with us."

Sharon grimaced but waved as she walked away.

Brian said, "So I see you've accepted the calling."

"How did you know?" Allison asked.

"The pickled squash gave it away," he said. "The bishop has been giving them out as bonuses to people who accept callings. He's no fool, either. He waits until they accept the calling before he brings it out."

"Do I get to give it back when I'm released?" she asked.

"We can always hope," he said.

A few minutes later with everyone's tears dried and all tucked away in their classes or quorums Allison set off in search of Sister Benson.

She found her in the Primary room straightening up chairs. "Hi, Maggie," Allison said. She sat down in one of the chairs. "Which of my children is it this time? Or was it Brian this morning?"

Maggie laughed. "That poor man. I tried but I couldn't get to him in time to tell him about the Sunbeam hats. But Primary survived. Did he?"

"Don't worry," Allison said. "He deserved it after what he just helped the bishop do to me."

Maggie sat down next to Allison and started looking serious. "Actually what I wanted to talk to you about is not a problem. In fact, it's very sweet of Andrew if we can figure out how to do it."

"What is it?" Allison asked puzzled.

"Well," Maggie began. "We were practicing for the sacrament meeting program we're having next Sunday and when it was Andrew's turn to do his part he came up to me and told me that he wanted to share his part with Melinda. He said he had asked her and she had said that she wanted to be in the program."

"Hmmm," Allison said.

"I told him I had asked you about Melinda being in the program before we started and you had said that she wouldn't do it, but he insisted that she wanted to do it so I told him I would ask you."

"Oh," Allison said and started thinking. Maggie waited expectantly.

When Allison finally spoke she said, "I don't know what to do. I just don't think that Melinda will go up in front of all those people and do anything. I can't even get her to stay in church without crying. But she does love Andrew and he's so good to her that I don't want to turn him down."

"Well, whatever you decide will be fine with me," Maggie said. A couple of children came into the room and she stood up. "We'd love to have Melinda in the program and even if she did get upset it certainly wouldn't hurt anything."

"I'll give you a call this week and let you know then," Allison said.

There was only one thing to do she decided as she walked down the hall. Let Brian help her decide whether to break Andrew's heart or let Melinda ruin the program. He made just that kind of heartbreaking decision every day in the tax business.

5

"So what should we do?" Allison asked Brian as they cleaned off the dinner table a while later. The three younger children were settled down for naps. Sharon had fled the kitchen, mumbling something about writing in her journal, and Andrew was sitting amid a pile of magic markers and paper in the middle of the family room floor.

"Do about what?" Brian asked. He was basically sitting at the table and handing her the dirty dishes to do.

"About Andrew and Melinda and the sacrament meeting program," she said.

"Oh." He scraped a few potatoes off a plate before he answered. "Why don't we just talk to him and tell him that even though Melinda says she wants to be in the program deep down she doesn't mean it. He knows what she's like in new situations and he'll understand."

"Who'll understand what, Dad?" Andrew walked into the kitchen with a stack of papers in his hands.

"You'll understand, son," Brian said. "Here — let us talk to you a minute." He pulled out a chair and patted the seat. "What do you have there?" he asked as Andrew put the papers down on the table.

"These are the cards I'm making for Melinda so she can learn her part for the program," Andrew said.

"Oh." Brian looked over at Allison who suddenly stopped putting the dishes in the dishwasher and looked up at him.

"That's sort of what we wanted to talk to you about, Andrew," Brian said. "Do you really think that Melinda wants to be in it? You know she doesn't even like church very much and she gets scared when you push her into new situations quickly."

"I know that, Dad," Andrew said. "That's why I thought we could go to church and practice with her one day after school so she'll know what to do. You could take us, couldn't you, Mom?"

"But, honey," Allison said. "you know that Melinda doesn't speak very clearly yet and everyone might not be able to understand her. Then she might start crying."

"I know that, too, Mom," he said patiently. "That's why I made these cards for her — to help her practice."

Brian picked up the cards and read them. "My family loves me."

"Do you think she can say all those words, Mom?" Andrew asked.

Allison glanced at Brian who was looking at the ceiling. She sat down and picked up the cards. "Well, she has a lot of trouble getting her lips together for an m and an f. And sometimes her l's sound more like m's."

"That's okay," Andrew said. "I bet if we practice a lot we can teach her how to close her lips okay."

"But Andrew, honey," Allison said. "We don't want you to get your hopes up and then have Melinda refuse to go up there and say her part."

"She won't, Mom." He got up and gathered up his cards. "Don't you think I'm going to pray about this?"

"We're sure you will, son," Brian said. "Just don't get your hopes up, okay?"

Andrew looked at both of them intently, but didn't say anything before he walked out of the room.

"This must have something to do with that scripture about the faith of a little child," Brian said. He looked at Allison and handed her a stack of dishes.

Allison only sighed despondently as she took the dishes from him. She put them down on the counter none too gently and went to stand before her calendar on the bulletin board. When this week could she fit in a trip to the church to practice?

She chose Monday. This way, she thought as she pushed Melinda into the chapel, she could show Andrew before he got too involved that this just would not work. Then they could praise him at Family Home Evening tonight and she could stop worrying about this and get on with worrying about Young Women's.

"You two can be the audience," she said to Matthew and Mark as she settled them on the front pew.

"Can we hip-hip-hooray, Mommy?" Mark asked.

"No," she said quickly. "Just sit there and practice being reverent." Not that they needed the practice ...

"Hip-hip-hooraying is more fun," Mark said.

"Okay," she relented. After all, they were missing Sesame Street for this. "Maybe just a teeny tiny hip-hip-hooray when she says her part. A real reverent-sounding one."

They immediately started whispering back and forth so she turned her attention back to Melinda. She had had a good day at school but had been so excited when Allison had told her where they were going after her nap that she decided not to take one. Allison saw no way this practice would work.

"Okay, Andrew," Allison said. "I'll sit here with Melinda and when you are ready to start you come and push her up front to say her part."

Andrew held his cards out to Melinda. "Do you need to see these again?" he asked her.

Melinda looked over at her mother and shook her head slowly.

"Then just do it the way you did yesterday at home," he said. "Okay?"

"Okay," Melinda said.

Allison gave her a little squeeze on the arm and tried to look excited.

"Here I come, Mom," Andrew said.

"Come on," she said.

He came over and very carefully let off the wheelchair brakes and pushed Melinda up front. She was still smiling.

He turned the wheelchair around so she faced the rows of pews, then stood beside her. "My family loves me," he said slowly.

She tried to repeat it after him but she was smiling so much with the excitement of the moment that her whole body became even tighter and her speech less clear.

"What do you think, Mom?" Andrew asked.

"Give it another try," Allison said. Why hadn't Melinda cried?

"Okay, Melinda," he said. "Try again and say it just as clear as you can. My family loves me."

Allison couldn't believe her ears. Melinda did try again and it sounded good. The m sort of disappeared by the end of the sentence but loves and family were almost clear.

Andrew was delighted and gave Melinda a big hug. Allison heard some hip-hip-hoorays from the back of the chapel.

"Did you hear that, Mom?" Andrew said. "She did it."

"Yes, honey, that was wonderful." She didn't feel wonderful, though. She felt a little disappointed and then she immediately felt guilty about feeling disappointed. She didn't want Melinda to fail and she didn't want Andrew to be heartbroken but she knew it was going to happen eventually so it should happen now and get it over with.

"Would you like to try again?" she asked Andrew.

"Nope," he said. "I think that's enough for today. After all, we have the rest of the week."

"You're right, Andrew," she said. And from where she stood it looked like an awfully long week.

6

*B*rian was late coming home that night, so Allison had to handle Family Home Evening without him. She was putting to bed what seemed like the last of twenty children when she heard the front door and then the closet door open and close. "Good night, Mark. Good night, Matthew. I love you and I don't want to hear another word from you until morning." She closed their door halfway, then peeked across the hall to make sure Melinda was still asleep. Allison always checked on Melinda throughout the night.

She was still asleep, so Allison walked quietly down the hall, snapped off the light, and called softly, "Brian, where are you?" He usually came in to tell the children good night if they weren't already asleep.

She heard a muffled voice say something that sounded like, "I'm in here."

"Where?" she asked. She headed in the direction of his answer and found him on his hands and knees halfway in the coat closet. "If this is a game of hide-and-go-seek, I just found you," she said.

He backed out of the closet until he was in the hallway, still on his hands and knees. "It isn't a game. My briefcase came open when I put it down and a bunch of papers fell out. I got down to pick them up and now I can't get up because my back is killing me." He looked up at her, smiling weakly. "I think I need a new briefcase."

"I think you need a new back." She pulled on his arm to help him up but he groaned.

"Just let me crawl by myself. Where do you want me?"

"The family room," she said. "You've got to see a doctor, Brian." He turned himself slowly around and she followed him.

When they got there she sat down on the couch as he collapsed on the floor beside it. She threw him a pillow and repeated, "You've got to go to a doctor, honey."

"I will. If I don't get better soon I will."

She didn't say anything to that because at the rate he was deteriorating one day soon she could just push him into the wheelbarrow and haul him away to the hospital. And he would be helpless to do anything about it.

"So how was Melinda's practice today?" he asked.

"She did it," Allison said wearily. "She didn't scream, cry, or even act afraid. I couldn't believe it."

"That's great."

"No, it isn't."

"It isn't?"

"No," she said. "Now Andrew has his hopes all up and I just don't think she'll do it on Sunday."

"Maybe she'll surprise us," Brian said. Then, "What's for supper?"

"Hamburger surprise."

"That's great," he said again, this time with somewhat less enthusiasm.

Allison threw another pillow at him. "No, it isn't," she said.

*

By Friday they had practiced two more times at the church and Brian's routine had changed. He didn't even bother to bring his briefcase in but headed right for the couch and lowered himself gently onto it. Not even a kiss. He just yelled, "Hi, honey. How's the project coming?"

Allison came in from the kitchen where she was mopping up orange juice. "Pretty good," she said. "Her speech teacher sent a note home today and said that Melinda had done a good job when they worked on it this afternoon." She bent down to kiss him.

"So you're convinced now that she will be the star of the show?"

"Maybe."

"That sounds convinced," he said. He sniffed in her direction. "Are you wearing a new perfume? You smell different."

"It's a citrus scent," she said. "Matthew spilled orange juice all over me and the floor." She sat down in the chair beside him. Usually she waited for him to ask but tonight she decided to jump right in. "I had a terrible afternoon."

He picked up her hand to hold. "What happened?"

"The boys wouldn't take a nap."

"That's reason enough."

"Then a spoon got stuck in the garbage disposal and a block got stuck in the vacuum cleaner. I took it apart and then lost the screws to put it back together."

"This sounds like one of your better afternoons, Allison." He started searching on the floor for the newspaper.

Allison pushed the paper farther away with her foot and tried to look mysterious to recapture his waning interest. "It gets more interesting," she said. "Sister Spence called me to see when we could get together to talk about Young Women so she could give me the books and talk about certain things." She paused dramatically.

"Yes?" he finally asked.

"She told me that as soon as I was sustained Sunday I would be getting a desperate phone call from Liz Moore."

"And?" This time he was really interested.

"It seems that she is worried to death that Ashley is going to marry Jared as soon as they graduate in the spring and she bugged Sister Spence the whole time she was the president to do something about them."

"Like what?"

"That's what she could never figure out but Liz kept calling anyway."

"Hmmm," Brian said. "Dan has never said anything about that." Dan was the other counselor in the bishopric. "But then I wonder sometimes if Dan ever gets to say anything in that marriage."

"That's not very nice," she said. She was thoughtful a minute, then said, "I guess I won't tell Liz how old we were when we got married."

He laughed at that and agreed. "So when are you going to get together with her?"

"Next Monday. If I wait until then I can still hope that someone will move into the ward who has "Young Women President" written all over her."

"Honey, I think you were made for the calling." He stretched for the newspaper but groaned in pain.

She picked it up and shoved it at him. "Here. Bury yourself in the sports section. Our conversation just ended."

"I have some news you'll like," he said casually.

She was walking out of the room but turned around when he said that. "What?"

"I have a doctor's appointment Monday morning."

"Oh, honey, that's wonderful." She walked back to the couch and threw her arms around him.

He put his newspaper down and carefully pulled her down beside him. "Maybe I should have made a doctor's appointment before now."

*

Saturday morning had been designated as dress rehearsal. Brian's condition gave him no choice but to babysit with the cheering section while Allison took Melinda and Andrew to church. Andrew even put a tie on and requested that Melinda wear a dress.

"Now don't let the boys stay in front of cartoons all morning," she said. She struggled to put a jacket on Melinda's unwilling arms. Brian was on the couch with the Saturday morning edition of the newspaper and the boys were playing on the floor with at least three thousand assorted blocks. "And stay on the couch so you will be able to go to church tomorrow." She zipped Melinda up. "And fix them a sandwich or something if we're gone too long."

He looked puzzled. "How can I fix lunch without getting off the couch?"

"Be creative," she said. "Taking care of children requires creativity."

"I'll do my best," he said. He waved good-bye to Melinda. "You do a good job for Daddy now."

"Bye-bye, Dada," she answered.

"Bye-bye, Daddy," Allison said too. She threw him a kiss then opened up the front door. As she backed the wheelchair out she heard Brian say, "Okay, boys, what channel are the Ninja Turtles on?"

A few minutes later she was backing the wheelchair into the church. The building was so quiet and peaceful that she wished it would feel the same way in the morning to keep Melinda calm. She had already planned — if they got that far — to keep Melinda out in the foyer until the sacrament was over and then wheel her in quietly when the program was announced.

"Okay, Mom," Andrew called from the chapel. "Sacrament's over and it's time."

"Let's go, sweetie," Allison said to Melinda. She pushed her through the doors and up the aisle. She sat down in a pew on the right and Andrew came over to push Melinda up front.

"Hey, Mom," he said as an idea hit him. "Do you think we could turn on the microphone and practice with that? Just once?"

Just because she was feeling a tiny bit of assurance and anticipation for the program Allison said, "I suppose so. After all, this is dress rehearsal and it will be on tomorrow." She regretted her decision almost instantly. When Andrew pushed the button the microphone let out the loudest and shrillest squeal Allison had ever heard. Andrew jumped back, putting his hands over his ears. Melinda jerked back in her wheelchair and flung her arms out. She started screaming just as loudly as the microphone. Her eyes opened wide with fear as she looked desperately around at Allison.

Allison jumped up, yelling at Andrew to turn the microphone off. But when he reached for it he hit it instead and it fell onto the stand with a bang. Melinda screamed even louder.

Allison finally reached the stand and yanked up the microphone, fumbling for the button. After an eternity she pushed it up and the squealing stopped. But as Melinda's screaming went on Allison knew that she was out of control and it would take a major effort to calm her down.

"Gosh, Mom," Andrew said. "That was loud."

Allison quickly unbuckled Melinda's seat belt and grabbed her up. Rubbing her on her back, she spoke soothingly. "It's okay, Melinda. It's all gone." Melinda screamed on.

Andrew came over and patted Melinda, too. "I'm sorry, Melinda. If you'll be quiet we can practice."

"Honey, I think practice is over with. It's going to take her a while to calm down." If she ever does, Allison thought. When Melinda was totally panicked she could scream for an hour or more.

Allison spent the next few minutes walking back and forth, patting, singing, and talking softly. Melinda screamed on. Finally she said, "Andrew, why don't you put our things in the wheelchair and push it out to the car? Maybe if we leave and go get a milkshake or something it will make her happy." She grabbed up Melinda's jacket, threw it around her, and started back down the aisle.

A chocolate milkshake later Melinda was not much better. Andrew ran off in the direction of his bike when they pulled up in the driveway and Melinda broke into high-pitched screaming again.

Brian was waiting at the front door by the time Allison pushed her up the sidewalk. "What happened?" he asked.

"The microphone squealed," Allison said. Melinda screamed even louder at the memory.

He came out on the porch and scratched Melinda on the head. "Hey, dollbaby," he said. "It's okay. You're home now and we don't have a loud old microphone."

She didn't stop.

"You're losing your touch," Allison said.

"I'll take her for a walk," he offered.

"You can't do that. You're in pain."

"I can do it. I'm fine." He took the wheelchair from Allison and started down the ramp. "We'll be back in a minute. She wants her Daddy."

Allison was spreading peanut butter on bread and dodging paper airplanes when she heard Brian and Melinda come in. Melinda was quiet. Brian was singing, "Hi-ho, hi-ho, it's off to bed we go." Allison stayed in the kitchen because when Melinda was this upset Brian could do more with her than Allison could.

After she sat the boys down at the table with their sandwiches and bananas she tiptoed into the family room and collapsed on the couch. She could hear Brian droning on in his reading voice. She didn't hear anything from Melinda.

She had almost dozed off when he came tiptoeing down the hall and stood in front of her. "Do you know how long those Care Bears books are?" he said.

"Long."

"I think she fell asleep out of self-defense," he said. He eased himself onto the couch beside her. "So how has Andrew taken this?"

"He hasn't said much," Allison said. "He helped me get everything in the car at church. And, of course, he had a milkshake. Then he was sort of quiet in the van but he ran out to play when we got home and didn't say a word about the program."

"He's probably so disappointed that he doesn't want to talk about it."

"Probably," Allison said. "But he can be proud of himself — he did a good job practicing. We'll just tell him that maybe by next year she'll be able to do it."

"He'll get over it," Brian said. "He's really a great kid."

"I'll bake him a cake tomorrow."

The front door banged shut just then. Andrew came into the living room, stopped, and looked around the room. "Did Melinda get quiet?"

"Finally," Brian said.

"Good," Andrew said. "Because she was crying so loud I forgot to tell you something."

"What?" Brian asked.

Allison took Brian's hand and squeezed it. She knew that together they could help Andrew get through this disappointment with his self-esteem and faith intact.

"Are you conducting tomorrow?" Andrew asked.

"Yes." Brian was solemn, a pillar of strength.

"Good, because I want you to make sure that tomorrow morning the microphone doesn't make a noise when you turn it on," Andrew said. "We don't want Melinda to get scared again and not be able to say her part. Will you promise me?"

It was quiet for just a moment while Brian and Allison looked at each other and sighed.

Then Brian said seriously, "I give you my word, son."

7

*A*nother Sunday morning at church she dreaded. This is getting to be a habit Allison thought as she laid Melinda back against the pillows on her bed and sat down beside her. She picked up Melinda's hand, swinging it back and forth. Melinda was preoccupied with hitting a stuffed kangaroo on the other side of her.

Usually Allison dressed the little boys and Sharon helped out with Melinda on Sunday mornings, but after intense negotiations around the breakfast table Sharon had agreed to dress the boys for the program this morning. It was going to cost Allison three dollars.

One of the terms of the settlement Sharon had insisted upon was the dreaded "lockup." When Allison had spent one Saturday at a particularly long Relief Society meeting a few months before, Brian had been inspired to reverse the locks on the boys' bedroom door. His inspiration had something to do with the black paint stain on the garage floor and the neighbor's dog but Allison hadn't asked for the details. So far neither Brian or Allison had felt inspired to change the locks back. The "lockup" had come in handy in many moments of extreme desperation.

Sharon had believed this morning to be such a moment. She had not wanted to chase her brothers all over the house so she insisted that Allison lock the door and let them out only when they were completely ready. It had been hairy the first couple of minutes but all seemed to be quiet down the hall in their room now. Maybe, for once, her total attention could go to Melinda.

Allison kissed Melinda's fist, "Do you feel sick this morning, honey?" she asked hopefully.

Melinda turned away from the kangaroo and shook her head.

Allison felt her forehead. She wasn't feverish. She felt her arms. She wasn't having chills either.

"Can you open up your mouth real wide and let Mommy see your throat?"

Melinda thought that was funny and laughed.

"Silly girl," Allison said. She tickled Melinda's stomach. "Do you think your Mommy's funny?"

Melinda laughed again.

"I guess I am being silly. I know you're not sick." She may as well face reality and dress her.

The night before Allison had laid out Melinda's prettiest dress for her to wear. It was a beautiful pink one with a lacy white apron. She had even bought her new barrettes with long ribbons that exactly matched the pink in the dress. With pink tights and white shoes on Melinda looked like a pretty little doll.

Allison fluffed and straightened until there was nothing left to fluff or straighten. She laid Melinda back again then stood up to survey her efforts. "What a pretty girl you are," she said. Melinda smiled her thanks.

As she put the brush back on the nightstand she saw Melinda's word cards. Andrew had brought them in before he left for church and asked Allison if she would go over them with Melinda one more time.

She picked them up but wasn't sure she wanted to remind Melinda of the day before in case she started screaming again. If Melinda did start crying it would mean she couldn't be in the program and then Allison would feel guilty because she would feel so relieved, but then Brian would accuse her of sabotage and she would wonder if he was right. But if she didn't go over her part with her and Melinda forgot it then she would feel guilty for not doing it and Andrew would blame her. There was no guilt-free choice.

The decision was taken out of her hands, though. There was suddenly the loud banging of fists against a door and screams of "let us out, let us out" coming from down the hall. Since it was Sharon doing the banging and screaming Allison thought she'd better get there quickly. She put the cards down, shoved a doll beside Melinda to keep her occupied, and raced down the hall.

"What's wrong, honey," Allison asked Sharon who had collapsed in Allison's arms. The boys looked like they were fully dressed. They were looking at something in a box on the bed between then.

Sharon pointed dramatically to the bed. "I hate those things," she said.

"Don't talk about your brothers that way," Allison said.

"Not them," Sharon said. "There. In the box."

Allison stepped back. She didn't like crawly things in boxes either. "What is it, Mark?"

"Just alligators. Bobby-down-the-street gave them to us," Mark said. He held the box out. Sharon shrieked.

"Don't panic, Sharon," Allison said. "He means caterpillars." Thank goodness it was caterpillars — she could run faster than them and they couldn't jump. "Can you take the box outside very carefully and let the caterpillars out? I bet their mommies are looking for them." She said it in the sweetest mommy voice she had.

"Okay, Mom," Mark said. "He looks a little homesick."

Allison and Sharon stepped back into the hallway as the boys marched past with box in hand. Sharon shrieked again. Then she grabbed Allison's arm and said, "I still get my three dollars, don't I?"

This Sunday they were almost late. Allison tried to get by Brother Wingate and stake out her place on the foyer couch before any mother with fussy babies got there, but she didn't make it. "Good morning, Brother Wingate," she said. She pulled her hand away as quickly as she courteously could and reached down to pick up Melinda's arm and point it toward him to save time. "Say hello, Melinda."

"Hi," Melinda said.

"Hello, Sister Lewis," he said to Melinda. "You look pretty today." He turned back to Allison, who was backing away an inch at a time, dragging the wheelchair toward the still empty couch. "We don't have any programs left. I'm sorry."

"That's okay." She was almost there. He was following her.

"I think your husband has one, though."

"That's just fine." She finally reached the couch and dropped the diaper bag on it. She still had to brush Melinda's hair and calm herself down. She heard Brian announce the opening hymn and hoped that Sharon had gotten Mark and Matthew to their right seats with their Primary classes in the chapel.

"I guess you could have my program, Sister Lewis. My wife has one."

"No, that's fine, Brother Wingate. You'd better hurry or you'll miss the opening hymn." She hoped he liked to sing.

"Okay," he said. "If you're sure about the program."

"I'm sure. Thanks anyway."

"See you later then." He shook Melinda's hand endlessly before walking away. Finally.

Why hadn't she taken that yoga class at the YWCA last year? Then maybe she would know how to do some magic breathing technique to slow her racing heart and dry up her sweaty palms.

"Hold your head up, Melinda," Allison said. She wiped her daughter's mouth and brushed her hair again. The opening hymn was over and someone was praying. Allison held Melinda's arms together and bowed her own head. Please don't let Melinda cry, she prayed silently. And don't let the microphone squeal or the boys cheer, she added.

She thought she was beginning to relax. She smiled at Melinda. Then she heard her name being offered up for a sustaining vote to be Young Women President. Oh no, she had forgotten all about that this morning. Evidently this was an all justice, no mercy morning.

She strained to hear Brian's verdict or any Young Women voices objecting. Then in one quick instant it was all over. She heard the word "unanimous" and she was officially sustained.

She slumped back against the couch and saw her future flash before her eyes. She stayed slumped until she heard the first notes of the sacrament hymn. Then she jumped up so fast that Melinda jumped.

"I'm sorry, honey," she said with as much calmness as she could pretend to. She had to get Melinda away from that sacrament hymn. "Would you like to go for a walk?" She jerked the brakes off and pulled the chair around so quickly that Melinda thought it was funny and laughed. Thank goodness she chose laughter.

Allison pushed her quickly down the hall, chattering away the whole time. She reached the ladies bathroom and pushed Melinda through the heavy doors. When they got inside Allison turned on all the water faucets and pushed on the hand blower to drown out any singing.

It worked so well she could hardly hear herself as she knelt down and started singing the Sesame Street theme song to Melinda. Melinda looked puzzled, then her eyes got real big as she looked toward the mirrors.

"Oh-oh," Melinda said. She looked at Allison and then back up again. Allison followed her gaze and saw what she saw.

All of the mirrors were dripping with steam.

"Oh no," Allison said. "My hair will frizz." She grabbed the diaper from the back of the wheelchair and put it on top of her head. Then she quickly turned off all the faucets. Melinda was thoroughly enjoying the show.

The hand blower mercifully shut off as Allison pulled Melinda back through the doors. Melinda was still laughing.

All Allison heard from the chapel was a quiet hush so she knew the sacrament was being passed. She walked down the hall with as much dignity as she could muster, patting Melinda on the shoulder as she went to calm her down. Reaching the couch, she sank down gratefully, then realized she still had the diaper on her head. She yanked it off, shaking her head at Melinda. "Forget you ever knew me, Melinda."

Suddenly the doors were opened. A lot of people in the chapel were coughing quietly. Sacrament was over.

Allison took a deep breath as she stood up. "This is it, sweetie. Are you ready?" Melinda nodded her head.

Allison barely heard Brian announcing the program as she walked down the aisle. She saw Andrew looking back at her just to make sure they had come. And she thought she saw everyone in the chapel staring at her as she headed for the empty seats ahead.

Her face felt hot as she sat down. She pulled Melinda as close to her as she could and wiped her mouth again as Melinda smiled at all the people and listened to her Daddy talk.

Since Melinda's part was at the end Allison tried to concentrate on the rest of the program. It wasn't any easier this year, though, to hear the children in Melinda's class sing and say their parts so easily and clearly. A familiar pang came to her heart as she remembered what Melinda should be able to do at her age. Seeing children Melinda's age was one of the most difficult times for Allison.

She glanced over at Melinda to see if she was upset seeing her Primary class up there but she was enthralled with the program. Then she looked over at Andrew who felt her gaze and returned her look. She smiled faintly at him and he flashed her an "okay" sign with his thumb and forefinger together. She knew then that she hadn't fooled him one bit that week with her forced enthusiasm.

It was their turn. Andrew walked solemnly over to Melinda, then pushed her more carefully than he ever had before and got in line behind the boy whose part came before theirs.

Not only had the smile left Melinda's face but her eyes had doubled in size. Here come the tears, Allison thought, and primed herself to go get her.

"My family teaches me about the gospel," the little boy in front of them said.

The bishop leaned over and helped push the wheelchair. Allison was surprised that didn't scare Melinda to death.

Andrew pulled the microphone down as close as he could to Melinda as Allison closed her eyes and waited for the squeal.

"Brothers and sisters," Andrew said. No squeal. "My sister is going to help me with my part."

Allison's lips froze in a smile in case anyone turned to look at her.

"Here it is," Andrew said. "My family loves me."

He looked down at Melinda and said, "It's your turn. Say my."

And then to the surprise of Allison, Melinda said, "My."

Andrew looked down at her again and said, "Family."

Melinda said, "'Amly."

"You didn't say your *f*. Say 'family'," Andrew whispered into the mike. Allison could feel the congregation smile.

Melinda took a deep breath and put her lips together with deliberation. A barely audible *f* came out, and, a split second later, the rest of the word.

"Good girl," Andrew said. "Loves me."

Just then the bishop coughed. Melinda jumped. Allison's heart sank.

Andrew scowled at the bishop. "Loves me," he repeated.

Melinda looked at Andrew and said "wuvs me" clearer than she had ever said it before.

Allison breathed a sigh of relief even as her eyes filled with tears. She noticed that several other people were wiping their eyes, too. Andrew was very collected, though, and matter-of-factly got behind the wheelchair and pushed Melinda away from the microphone. Then he turned back to the mike and announced, "We do love her, you know."

Yes, we do, Allison wanted to shout to everyone. And we love you, too, Andrew, she thought as she watched him carefully wheel Melinda back to her place and then return to his seat.

Allison reached over to give Melinda a squeeze and told her that she had done a great job. Melinda smiled back at her, and kept on smiling as if she never meant to stop. Allison kept glancing over at Andrew, but he was paying close attention to the rest of the program and didn't look over a single time.

When the amens were said and the organ began the postlude Allison went over to Andrew and gave him a big hug. "You did a great job, son. We're so proud of you."

"Didn't Melinda do a great job, too, Mom?" he asked.

"She sure did. And she couldn't have done it without a brother like you."

"Just think, Mom, next year she can say a whole big piece. Maybe even give a talk or something."

Allison reached down to hug him again, then held him back and looked down into his eyes. "Let's give her a year and see, Andrew."

Then she thought, Let's give me a year and see how much of a little child I've grown into by that time, too.

8

*U*sually Allison's feelings about the day ahead of her matched the way she felt about the laundry when she opened the bathroom closet where it was kept hidden from the general public. If she was excited about what faced her that day she felt challenged by the laundry. If she was tired or worried about something — it didn't take much — she felt burdened by the massive pile of twisted soggy clothes.

The Monday after the sacrament meeting program, though, she really couldn't define her feelings. She was still elated about the way the program had turned out but then she was apprehensive about her meeting with Sister Spence later that morning. Then there was Brian's doctor's appointment and that could go either way. Hopefully, the doctor had some miracle medicine to take his pain away. But then the doctor could say Brian could never work again and she would have to support the family. And she was sure the only job available would be doing laundry.

It was no use. She couldn't decide on any definite feeling so she grabbed up all the towels and shoved them into the clothes basket. She could wash towels without any commitment. At any point along the laundry process towels could be forgotten without wrinkling. And with all the towels still in the closet no one was likely to say "Where's the towel I was going to use tonight" like they did with shirts and dresses. So towels it was.

After she made sure the amount of towels, water, detergent, bleach, and fabric softener was delicately balanced she went in search of Brian. He was supposed to be leaving in a few minutes for his appointment.

She found him shaving. "You're going to be late," she said.

"No, I'm not."

She leaned against the door and picked up his towel to hold for him. "Are you sure you don't want me to go with you? He might give you some medicine that you're not supposed to drive with."

"Well, then, I'll just take it when I get home," he said. "You have that meeting, remember?"

"I remember," she said. "But I'd rather go with you."

Eyes closed and face dripping, Brian fumbled around for something on the sink. "Where's my towel?"

"Here, I was holding it for you." She shoved it into his hands and began picking up the things he had knocked off the sink. "Are you sure?"

"I'm sure," he said. "Now if you'll just let me by I have to go. I'm going to be late as it is." He pecked her cheek, then gently moved her aside to get through the door.

She followed him down the hall and to the front door. "Will you call me if they decide to amputate your back?"

"You'll be the first to know," he said. "But I imagine he'll give me some kind of muscle relaxer or something."

And he was gone. Allison turned back to the living room and viewed the mess that meant Monday morning. It always amazed her how a home could look so neat and clean at six-thirty in the morning when she first saw the living room and a mere seven breakfasts, four packed lunches, one carpool, one bus, one minibus, and assorted lost shoes, books, and papers later it could look like it did now. As she picked up she decided that she should be the one with back problems since she spent half her time bent over picking up after people.

Suddenly, she was attacked from behind by two little boys in Superman pajamas. She landed on the pillows she had been putting back on the couch like they always were in the magazines so her fall wasn't too painful. Reaching around, she grabbed the boys and pulled them onto her lap. She couldn't resist little boys in pajamas. "Hi, boys," she said. "How did my two little Supermen sleep?"

"I don't know, Mommy," Mark said. "I was asleep."

Matthew grabbed her around the neck and buried his face in her shoulder. "Hi, sweetie," she said to him. "Are you hungry? What would you like for breakfast?"

"Krispies," he said, like he always did.

"Okay, I can handle that. What would you like, Mark?"

"Superman only eats green kryptonite," he said. "Is it okay with you if we fly to the kitchen?"

"Sure, be my guest," she said. She pulled herself up off the floor and, even though she knew it was useless, lined up all the pillows again before following the boys to the kitchen.

As she poured out Rice Krispies and stirred green food coloring into instant oatmeal her thoughts turned toward the meeting with Sister Spence. She didn't know why she dreaded it so much except that once you accepted lesson manuals and rollbooks from someone it was definite that you would be teaching a class. Without lesson manuals and rolls she still felt unofficial.

But if the bishop thought she could do it and Brian thought she could do it, maybe she could. She had already planned a get-acquainted game for the Young Women activity Wednesday night. All the girls would sit in a circle and spin a Sprite bottle. Then the girl the bottle pointed to would have to tell something about the girl who spun the bottle. Then everyone would giggle and love each other and think Young Women (and Allison) were a lot of fun. Allison had mentioned it to Sharon yesterday and she had said it sounded a little dumb but Sharon was at that age where she thought most everything Allison did was dumb.

Mark interrupted her thoughts with "What are we going to do today, Mommy?" He got a little bored when they stayed home all day.

"Well, Mommy has a meeting today so you two have to be quiet and good."

He rolled his eyes. "Oh no, not that again."

"But Daddy has the day off so maybe he'll feel better when he comes home from the doctor and can take you to the park to play."

"All right," Mark said. Matthew clapped his hands.

"For now, though, I'll clean up the kitchen while you two sit and eat all of your breakfast like good boys. Then we'll get you dressed and you can watch Sesame Street while I vacuum."

Mark considered her proposal a few seconds then said, "It's a deal, Mommy." Then he jumped down from his stool and out of the way of the river of Rice Krispies and milk heading his way from the bowl Matthew had just spilled.

Sister Spence drove up right on time at ten o'clock.

"Now, boys, remember to play quietly while Sister Spence is here." Allison had wanted Brian to be home by the time Sister Spence had come but she hadn't heard a word from him.

"We will, we will," Mark said. They had tied up their big fire engines with Sharon's old jump rope and were dangling them from the back of a chair. It might just have been her imagination but it seemed to Allison that they never played with anything the way the instructions instructed.

"Hi, Sister Lewis," Sister Spence said. She walked into the living room with a stack of books and papers. "Are you ready for all this?"

"I don't know," Allison said. "It looks like a lot of work."

Sister Spence sat down on the couch and unloaded her arms. "Well, it is a lot of work but it's also a lot of fun. You know, teenagers can really keep you hopping."

This was not what Allison wanted to hear. She wanted to hear something about blessings and rewards and girls loving you so much that they begged to wash windows and babysit.

Allison sat down on the other end of the couch with the books between them. "Should we pray before we start?" she asked.

"It wouldn't hurt," Sister Spence said.

"Would you like to offer it?" Allison asked. She needed all the prayers anyone would offer in her behalf.

As Sister Spence said "Amen" Matthew shouted "Mommy!" and Mark started screaming. Allison jumped up as Mark dragged Matthew into the living room.

Allison could already see a goose-egg rising on his forehead. She picked him up quickly. "What happened?"

"He crashed into my fire engine when it was swinging."

"Can you go get me some ice and a washcloth?" she asked Mark. As he went running Allison threw a pillow on the floor and tried to lay Matthew down. He screamed louder, though, and clung to her. She held him tighter and rocked him back and forth.

"You may as well start telling me everything I need to know, Sister Spence, because this is about as calm as it gets around here."

"Really?" she said. She had only one sweet daughter in college.

"Really." Mark was back with the ice. She wrapped it in the washcloth and put it on the lump. He howled. She tried unsuccessfully to convince him to let her hold the ice on his head but he wouldn't convince so she finally gave up and gave him the ice to suck on. It always worked out that way.

"Can I have some, too, Mommy?" Mark asked.

"If you will sit down and be quiet you can have some." She put Matthew down on the pillows. Mark ran out and was back quickly with the whole ice-tray. Allison put a pillow down for him, put the ice-tray between them and turned her attention back to Sister Spence. "So how many girls are there?" she asked.

Sister Spence pulled out a couple of papers and handed one to Allison. "There are twelve girls on record but only about eight come with any regularity."

Thank goodness for small wards, Allison thought. How many problems can eight girls have?

"But believe me," Sister Spence said. "These girls have enough problems for twenty."

Allison couldn't restrain herself any longer. "Oh no."

"Oh don't worry," Sister Spence said. She leaned over and patted Allison's arm. "You'll do fine. The girls are real sweet when you get to know them." She looked down at her list. "Let's see — you know Terri Lynn Parker, don't you?"

Raisins and pierced ears. "Yes."

"And Rhonda Rhodes?"

Raisins and pierced ears. "Yes."

"They're real sweet girls," Sister Spence said. "They are sort of the leaders in Young Women. All the girls want to be just like them and some of the parents worry about that. But I think they are basically harmless."

They were nice to Melinda. Allison was sure she could live with them.

"Then there is Jennifer McCleary. Sort of watch out for her. She's real smart and she loves to catch you wrong on anything." Sister Spence paused thoughtfully and then said, "I think she hated me actually."

Allison gulped. "Hated you?"

"Yes," Sister Spence said. "Ever since I caught her out back of the church smoking I've had the feeling she didn't like me."

"Smoking?"

"Yes, but don't worry about it. I don't think she does it anymore." She turned back to her list.

Allison drew some little swirls of smoke beside Jennifer's name.

"Let's see — Crystal Manning," Sister Spence continued. "You know her, don't you?"

"Usually surrounded by a crowd of boys?"

"I think the boys would prefer to have her with them at Young Men." Sister Spence looked down at her notes again and added, "Make sure she's there the nights you have lessons on the law of chastity."

Allison drew lips beside Crystal's name.

"And then there's Ashley Moore," Sister Spence began. She was interrupted by the phone ringing.

"Excuse me," Allison said. "I'll be right back." She glanced at the boys. They were down to their last ice-cube but she thought she had plenty of time to get the phone.

She was wrong. When she returned a few minutes later the boys were gone. "Where did my boys go?" she asked Sister Spence politely.

She looked up. "I think they said something about fixing refreshments for us."

"Oh no," Allison said, barely controlling her panic. "Mark? Matthew? Where are you?" She headed for the kitchen without waiting for an answer.

There were four graham crackers and two pieces of bologna lined up on the counter. Matthew was standing in the middle of the floor holding a knife that was dripping with grape jelly. Mark was kneeling down in front of him with a handful of napkins trying to wipe up the puddle of grape jelly at his feet.

"I sorry, Mommy," Matthew said. He looked pitiful with the huge lump on his forehead and tears in his eyes.

"He didn't mean to, Mommy," Mark said. "He's just a little guy."

"I know," Allison said. "And little guys can make big messes. That's why big guys like you should watch them," she said sternly. She took the extremely sticky knife away from Matthew and wet some paper towels. She handed them to Mark. "Clean it up."

"We thought you might be hungry," Mark said. "We were going to make lemonade but we couldn't find the hammer to smash the lemons."

That's something to be thankful for, Allison thought. She picked the lemons up off the floor and handed them each two graham crackers. "Why don't you two eat the graham crackers on the porch and wait for Daddy?"

"Will he take us to the park?" Mark asked.

"Let's hope so. Now go get your jackets and go outside."

When they were outside she went back into the living room. Sister Spence had made the pile on Allison's side of the couch larger than the one on her side.

"I'm sorry that took so long," Allison said.

"I think we were on Ashley Moore," Sister Spence said. She chewed on the end of her pen. "I can't believe her mother hasn't called you yet."

Then Allison remembered her phone call. "She just did."

Sister Spence leaned back against the couch and shook her head knowingly. Allison fell back against the couch and sighed despondently. "I can't do this."

"Of course you can, Sister Lewis. She's just a worried mother."

"More than just worried. I would say frantic and hysterical. She wants me to convince Ashley Wednesday night that she should never see Jared again, get inducted into the Honor Society, and not get married until she finishes law school. Or medical school. She's flexible on that."

"That sounds just like conversations I've had with her."

"Is Jared really that bad?"

"No. Jared is a wonderful boy. They've liked each other since they were Sunbeams. Liz is just afraid that they are going to get married next spring when they graduate. And the way they look at each other it just might happen."

"Oh no," Allison said again. "What am I going to do?"

"There's not much you can do. I just sort of listened to her and told her not to worry."

"I could say something about the Honor Society Wednesday night," Allison said. "I was a member in high school." Back before Big Bird had become her alter-ego.

"That leaves Erin Walker and you won't have any trouble with her. She's a lovely girl. Just lovely."

Allison put a smiley face beside her name.

"Now about Wednesday night. Has Sharon told you about what they had planned?"

"No," Allison said. "She hasn't said a word."

"You do know about the cake auction the ward is having Friday night?"

"Yes." Of course, she remembered. She had suggested it to Brian one day as a fun way to increase the ward budget. Would she now regret that suggestion?

"Well, the girls decided that they wanted to decorate cakes for it, so they were going to bring their cakes already baked to the activity Wednesday night and decorate the cakes together. It sounded like fun to me."

Maybe, Allison thought.

"Each of the girls donated two dollars to buy the decorating supplies and I was going to buy them before the meeting." She handed Allison an envelope of money and what seemed to be an incredibly long grocery list. "Is that all right with you?"

"I guess so," Allison said. Maybe she could run to the store later since Brian was home. Mark and Matthew made grocery shopping too exciting.

"And," Sister Spence continued. "My assignment was to make some decorator icing. So I copied the recipe down for you." She handed it to Allison.

Allison felt a glimmer of hope — just a small one — but there nevertheless. She had taken a cake decorating class several years ago. She even thought she knew where her kit was.

"Now for the manuals," Sister Spence said. "Here's one for each class." She handed the three manuals over. "By the way, I forget who your counselors are."

Her glimmer of hope sputtered and died. "No one yet," she said. "The bishop said it might take a while since there are so many callings and so few people available."

Sister Spence shook her head sympathetically. "Keep reminding him," she said. "You'll need counselors. Mine either moved or went inactive, so I *know*." It sounded awfully ominous to Allison.

It wasn't much longer before it was all over. There were no papers on Sister Spence's side of the couch. They all belonged to Allison now and her life was officially intertwined with the lives of the girls whose names she held in her hand.

Allison handed Sister Spence her coat and held the door open. She felt she had to give it one last try. "Are you sure you want to be released from this calling, Sister Spence? You seem to care so much about these girls."

"Oh, I do," she said. "But I know you'll do a wonderful job. And I love my new calling on the stake Primary board." She patted Allison on her arm. "Give yourself a little time and you'll feel like you have a whole new family of daughters."

Allison let that comment go in one ear and out the other as she shut the door. The boys were around back playing in the sandbox so she had a moment to lie in lonely depression on the couch. She went over to the stereo and caressed her Letterman album before putting it lovingly in its jacket. Then she yanked one of Sharon's Bon Jovi albums out of its jacket and turned it on. Not willing to show too much enthusiasm, she kept the volume low and lay down on the couch with the books at her feet. She felt incredibly old.

9

Allison was glad to hear Brian drive up before the album could get very far. As she walked to the door she could hear the happy shouts of the boys as they greeted their Daddy, but before she could open the door she heard the shouts turn to tears and sobs. She opened the door to find Brian coming up the walk with an arm around each unhappy boy.

"What's wrong?" She immediately thought of fingers mashed in car doors. But both of them?

"They wanted me to take them to the park but I told them I couldn't."

"You can't? Why not?"

Brian pushed the boys inside and Allison picked up Matthew. He clung to her shoulder and whimpered while Mark held onto Brian's legs and whined.

"The doctor said I have to go to bed the rest of the week."

"The rest of the week? What's wrong?" She plopped Matthew down on the couch then pried Mark away from

Brian's legs and put him down beside Matthew. "Would you boys please hush so I can hear what Daddy is saying?" "But we want to go to the park," Mark whined. "Well, sometimes we don't get what we want." She left it at that and followed Brian down the hall and into the bedroom where he was already shedding his clothes. "What's wrong with you?" she repeated. She sat down on the bed worried and concerned.

"He said it looks like I have a bulging disc."

"What's that?"

"Here's a book he gave me to read." He handed her a small booklet and explained. "Evidently the discs between the vertebrae in my back have squeezed out and are pushing on the nerves causing the pain. He said the best treatment is to stay in bed for several days and see if it improves. The only time I can get up is for occasional trips to the bathroom."

She looked up from the book. "Thank goodness for that."

He finished buttoning his pajama top and climbed into bed. "Are you mad?"

"Why would I be mad?" she asked. The idea of having him home all week appealed to her. They could talk. They could play trivia. Maybe, too, if he got an eye-witness view of how hard she had to work all day he would let her have someone in to help her clean once a week like he had talked about for so long. Well, she had talked about.

"I just hope it doesn't make things too hard on you," he said.

"Oh, I can manage," she assured him. She leaned over to kiss him. "It will be sort of nice to have you home all week where I can keep an eye on you." She smoothed his pillow. "But what are you going to do all week?"

"I thought I'd call the office in a little bit and have them bring some work over I can look at lying down." He yawned. "Right now I'd like to close my eyes, though. He gave me some pretty strong pain medicine and I'm getting sleepy."

"Okay," she said. "I'd better go see why the boys are so quiet anyway." She turned the sheet back over the blanket so the blanket wouldn't be rough on his face. "If you need anything just call. Do you want the TV on?"

"No," he said. "There's nothing on but game shows and soap operas."

She started out the door but turned back when he said, "Oh, I almost forgot. Can you go get my prescriptions filled?"

"Now?"

"If you can. I need to start on them as soon as I can." He buried himself again and mumbled. "They're on the dresser."

Allison picked up the prescriptions then looked at her watch. Twelve o'clock. If she hurried she could get the prescriptions, run to the grocery store, and be back in time to get the boys down for their naps and quiet before Melinda came home at one-thirty for her nap.

She found the boys still on the couch. Matthew was sucking his thumb and almost asleep. Mark was hiding under the cushions.

"Get up, Mark," she said. "You know you aren't supposed to take the cushions off the couch."

He popped up. "What's wrong with Daddy?"

"His back is hurting and the doctor told him to stay in bed for a couple of days." She scooped Matthew up and deposited him on a chair in the kitchen. "We have to go get some medicine for Daddy so I'll fix you two a sandwich to eat in the car. Do you want ham or baloney?"

"Ham," Mark said.

"Bony," Matthew said.

"Mark," she ordered. "Go get your coats. Matthew, take your thumb out of your mouth. You can't go to sleep yet."

Mark, evidently sensing the importance of the medicine mission, ran to obey. Matthew took his thumb out of his mouth just long enough to yawn, then put it back in.

By the time Mark returned Allison had two sand-wiches — crusts cut off — in two baggies. She shoved the crusts in her mouth for what would probably be her lunch and held the boys' coats for them.

"What sweet boys I have," she said. She zipped them up, pushed a sandwich in one hand and grabbed their other, and headed out the door.

Within an hour she had returned, Matthew asleep on her shoulder and Mark dragging a bag behind him. It took her only a few minutes with Mark helping to unload the groceries. Then she gave him the book she'd bought him at the store and sent him off to bed.

She followed him down the hall and peeked in on Brian. He was awake, staring at the ceiling. "I'm bored and hungry," he said. "Could I have some lunch?"

"Sure," she said. "I'll fix us a sandwich and we can eat together."

All the homemaking meetings she had ever attended flashed through her mind as she reached into her china closet and took out two of her best china plates. She dug out a silver tray from one of the drawers and decided that a few strategically placed napkins would hide the hints of tarnish. A china rose carefully pulled from her collection on the dining room table went into a bud vase.

She made two ham and cheese sandwiches with lettuce, tomato, mayonnaise and a hint of mustard just like Brian liked them. Then she unmercifully speared four olives with toothpicks and stuck them on the sandwiches. Next she alternated red and golden apple slices on a plate with grapes in the middle and filled two tall thin glasses she never let the children touch with lemonade. A bowl of potato chips for them to intimately share completed their lunch.

"Lunch is served," she announced grandly. She carefully put the tray down in the middle of the bed and stood back to bask in his admiration.

He didn't let her down. He whistled and said, "I'm impressed. What a woman!"

"It was nothing," she teased. "The little boys and I eat like this every day."

"Is this all for me?" he asked.

"Touch my sandwich and you're a dead man." She switched the channel on the TV and snapped it on before she sat down on the bed. The hourglass and tick-tocking that marked the beginning of "Days of Our Lives" came on.

"You don't still watch this, do you?" he asked. "I thought you gave up soap operas."

"I only watch one now," she said defensively. "And I'm going to give it up as soon as I find out who's in the red scarf."

Brian rolled his eyes and took a big bite out of his sandwich.

"So I'm weak," she said. "I have to do something exciting while I fold clothes." She picked up her sandwich and glanced over at the TV. "So how do you feel?"

"Fine, while I'm lying down."

"Do you want something to read? I could run to the library after Sharon gets home."

"No," he said. "I found this book on the nightstand." He held up the thick novel her sister had sent her for her birthday that she hadn't had a chance to even open yet.

"You lucky duck," she said. "Look — there's the woman in the scarf now."

"And you don't know who she is?" he asked.

"Nope."

He chewed a minute. "Who do you think she is?"

"I think it's Patch's first wife Marina, who supposedly died when he accidently pushed her overboard from the merchant marine ship."

"If she died, how could she come back?"

"Well," she said dramatically. "We've only seen flashbacks so far, but they probably never found her body. And now, just when Steve and Kayla were so happy after they missed being blown up in the computer cave, someone sends them a bottle of wine in the mail. Steve thinks it's from Marina even though he hasn't told Kayla yet."

"So where does Patch fit in?" His eyes were riveted to the screen.

"Oh, I'm sorry," she said. "Steve is Patch. He lost his left eye in a fight over his girlfriend Britta who was a KGB agent and he wore a black patch until he had to go undercover to see who was trying to kill his best friend, the plastic surgeon Marcus." She paused for a breath. "So they fixed him up with a glass eye."

"What a relief," Brian said.

"Don't patronize me, Brian. Give yourself time — you'll care, too."

"Never."

It was a commercial, so she picked up the tray and started from the room. She made it all the way to the door before Brian asked, "So — what's a computer cave?"

10

"Why do we have to have a picnic in your bedroom, Mom?" Sharon asked. "It sounds strange even for *your* Family Home Evenings."

"Because we have to keep Daddy's spirits up and he can't come to us so we'll go to him," Allison said.

"Does he want us?" Sharon asked.

"Of course he does." She put a loaf of french bread and a plate of devilled eggs down into the picnic basket she had won at a Tupperware party. Fried chicken and carrot sticks were already in there. "Andrew, can you push Melinda down the hall? Matthew, you get the napkins and, Mark, you take this tablecloth and spread it over Daddy's bed."

She led the parade down the hall and opened up the bedroom door. Brian was sitting up in bed watching "Name That Tune" in his red plaid pajamas. Allison walked into the room but quickly jumped back into the hall. "Andrew, keep Melinda out here just a minute." Andrew stopped quickly behind the wheelchair. Matthew and Mark crashed into him and down went all the napkins.

She pushed the bedroom door closed behind her and whispered loudly, "Brian, your pajamas!"

"Shh, he's about to win the Golden Roulette." He looked down at his pajamas. "What's wrong with my pajamas. I love these pajamas."

"I know. But remember — Melinda is afraid of them. If I bring her in here she'll scream bloody murder." Melinda was afraid of some of the strangest things but they had learned long ago to take her fears seriously. She had been afraid of cherry pie filling since someone had spilled some on her when she was a baby. And she'd been afraid of Brian's red pajamas since the morning he had stumbled into Melinda's room to get her up during a season of Allison's morning sickness and none had warned her what red and green plaid did to her Daddy's appearance.

"Well," Brian said. "Hand me my shirt and tie." They were still draped over the chair from that morning.

"Coast is clear," Allison said. In came the parade. Mark threw the tablecloth on the bed and Matthew threw the wrinkled napkins on top of it. Then they both jumped on the bed and toward their Daddy. He was lying on his side with his white shirt on backwards and his tie thrown around his neck.

"Hi boys," he said. "Don't jump on me." He turned to look at Melinda. "Hi, Babe. Did you come to see your Daddy?"

"Never let it be said of the Lewis family that we let a little thing like a sick father keep us from Family Home Evening." She spread out the tablecloth neatly and un-packed the food.

"She says it's a picnic, Daddy," Sharon said. She was sampling the cosmetic wares on Allison's dresser.

"We might be going to eat," he said. "But I doubt it's going to be a picnic."

"Where should I put Melinda, Mom?" Andrew asked.

"Brian?" Allison had hoped that Brian could manage to feed Melinda from his sickbed. "I can try," he said. "Give me her plate." He rolled over on his back and balanced his plate and Melinda's on his stomach. "Will you eat for Daddy?" She opened her mouth wide and he shoved a devilled egg in.

"Brian, you'll choke her!" Allison said.

"I can't see much from this position, Allison." He did not sound like he was enjoying the picnic.

Allison scraped the egg off Melinda's mouth and took the plate off his stomach. "I'll feed her."

The doorbell rang.

"Please," Sharon said. "Let me get it."

They listened as she answered the door and could hear a man's voice protesting and apologizing as Sharon insisted that he come on back to the bedroom. Allison and Brian looked at each other questioningly but couldn't tell who it was. The voices came closer until there was a soft knock at the bedroom door followed by Sharon's announcement that Bishop Murphy was there.

"Hi, come on in, Bishop," Allison said. She quickly wiped Melinda's mouth again and swallowed her mouthful she hadn't finished chewing.

Brian waved a friendly chicken leg and said, "Have a seat."

Bishop Murphy stood at the door with a foil-wrapped package in one hand and a letter in the other. He looked like he didn't quite know what he had interrupted.

"We're just having Family Home Evening," Allison explained. She looked at Brian lying there with his backwards shirt and untied tie, chicken leg in one hand and carrot stick in the other. Then there were two boys who had made guns out of their french bread to shoot each other. Sharon was standing behind him blocking any kind of escape. Allison felt a rush of sympathy for this poor man who for once had a real reason for his confusion. So she brushed crumbs off the bed to clear up a corner for him to sit on and gave him a mile-a-minute history of the last twenty-four hours and medically footnoted explanation of why Brian was in bed.

The bishop relaxed. He asked as she finished, "This is Monday night? It's felt like a Tuesday to me all day." He shook his head and looked down at his hands. "Oh, this is great about Brian." Then he caught himself. "I don't mean great about his back. I mean it's great that I came tonight and brought him something he can munch on in bed." He handed Allison the package.

It caught her off balance and she almost dropped it because it was at least ten pounds heavier than she had expected it to be. "Thank you, Bishop. This is real sweet of you." She didn't ask what it was. She didn't want to know.

"Sharon," she said. "Why don't you put this in the kitchen and we can eat it for dessert. Or breakfast."

"It's squash bread," the bishop said. "Whole wheat squash bread with poppy seeds in it, I think the wife said."

Behind him Sharon put her hand over her mouth and gagged.

Allison shot her a stern look and shoved the loaf toward her. "It sounds delicious."

It must have been Sharon's lucky night because the phone rang. "I'll get it," she shouted. She grabbed the loaf, picked up her plate, and backed out the door. "Bye, bishop, bye Dad, good-bye everyone."

Allison didn't even care about her hasty departure. The more distance between her and the squash bread the better.

"Is that letter for us, too?" she asked the bishop. If it was something important she didn't want him to forget it.

"Letter?" he asked.

"That letter," she said. She pointed to his hand.

"Oh, this letter," he said. He looked down at it, shaking his head. "Brian, you've got to help me." He sounded disconsolate and languishing. "I got a letter from the IRA."

"IRS?" Brian asked.

"Whatever." He sank to the corner of the bed and repeated, "You've got to help me."

Allison handed Brian the letter that the bishop held out to her. She didn't know whether to stay and carry on the picnic or leave her husband alone to comfort this poor distraught man. "Should I leave?" she asked Brian, who was reading the letter.

As he turned to answer her a chicken leg landed on the letter. "Mark!" he said. "Could you please calm down?"

"We'll leave," Allison said. She started throwing things back into the basket and pushed it toward Andrew who was sitting quietly on the floor eating. "Let's go to the kitchen, kids." She grabbed up the tablecloth, almost unseating the bishop.

She draped the tablecloth around Mark's neck and headed him out the door in the direction of the kitchen. This time down the hall she and Melinda brought up the rear of the straggly parade that dragged and dropped things all the way to the kitchen where they dumped everything on the kitchen table.

"Is the picnic over, Mommy?" Mark asked.

"I guess so," she said. "Just sit down and finish eating."

"Where's the chicken?" Andrew asked.

They searched but it was missing. And Allison hadn't even had a piece yet.

"We didn't have an opening prayer, Mom," Andrew said. "Did that still count as Family Home Evening?"

"It better," she said. "We're all family, we were all home, and it's six o'clock in the evening. It counts."

It seemed to Allison as she sat feeding Melinda little bites of bread that every time she spent almost a whole afternoon preparing a really great Family Home Evening, something went wrong. Sudden onsets of flu, broken collarbones, overflowing toilets, swarms of termites — they all happened during Family Home Evening.

"Mom!" Sharon's whisper broke into Allison's thoughts. She had unwrapped the squash bread and was looking at it with dismay as it lay yellow and heavy in her hands. "Mom, this looks really gross."

Allison looked at it, wrinkling up her nose. Then, because she was feeling a little bit sorry for herself and awfully hungry for the chicken held hostage in the bedroom where her husband was lying comfortably in bed she said, "Sharon, why don't you cut some of it and put it on a plate to take in to your Daddy and the bishop?"

11

*I*t did not occur to Allison until the next morning that it was not only her husband who was confined to bed, but also her babysitter for the first Young Women activity she was to preside over.

"But I hate to think that the first official thing I do as Young Women president is to cancel the meeting tomorrow night." She had fled to the bedroom to see Brian as soon as it occurred to her. "And they were going to decorate cakes for the cake auction Friday night."

"Get a babysitter," Brian suggested. "I'd be here to supervise."

"I don't have a babysitter that I can leave all the children with at that time of night. No one knows how to take care of Melinda for that long." It was true, too. Since Melinda had been born Allison had not left her with anyone except Brian for any length of time. No one really ever volunteered either. People who usually offered to babysit said things like, "I'd keep Melinda too but I don't trust myself taking care of her." So dates had mainly been late movies or home-delivered pizzas after the children were all in bed.

"Sharon could babysit," Brian said.

"Honey, she's a Young Woman." The only solution was to call the bishop and ask to be released. This was just the kind of situation she knew was going to happen when she had accepted the calling.

"Have the meeting here," Brian said. He was flipping channels with the TV remote control.

"Here?"

"Sure," he said. "Melinda could stay back here with me and you'd be here if she needed any standing-up thing to be done." He stopped on Phil Donahue. It was about the rights of women firefighters to sleep in the nude in the fire station.

"That just might work," Allison said. Her kitchen table was big enough for all the girls. And as long as they all helped clean up it couldn't be too much trouble. "That's a pretty good idea, Brian."

"You wouldn't think so if I was a firefighter."

"I mean having the meeting over here. It just might work." She walked over and flipped the TV dial until she found an old Green Acres rerun. "Thanks for suggesting it." She picked up the empty bottle of Pepto-Bismol off the nightstand. "Do you need anything before I go?"

"Yeah," he said. "If we have any family group sheets I'd like to have a few to work with. Do you have any?"

"I think so," she said. She was so glad that he was going to be doing something useful and uplifting that she'd be glad to resurrect some. He had watched more TV the last twenty-four hours than he'd watched in the last five years. "I'll bring them in as soon as I remember where I put them."

"No rush," he said. "I probably won't need them until this afternoon." Watching to see if she was leaving, he edged his hand toward the TV dial.

"Go ahead and change it. But," she warned, "don't ever ask to go to firemen's school."

"It never crossed my mind," he said. He crossed his heart with his finger and flipped the dial.

"You're watching too much TV," she said.

"I'm going to do some work as soon as the bishop brings over his tax information. He really messed up his taxes last year."

She couldn't imagine the bishop doing his own taxes. "I'm sure you'll be brilliant with him," she said, buttering him up. "Now could the boys stay in here with you — their father — while I make my frosting?"

"Sure, they like Price is Right."

"What else?" she said.

"Oh, I almost forgot," Brian said, consulting a note-pad. "Can you tell me the suggested retail price for the six-ounce package of rice-cakes and Boraxo hand-cleaner? I had no idea yesterday how much they cost. I would have lost a trip to Aruba."

"I'll think about it," she said. She shook her head as she walked down the hall. This was a Brian she had never known. If his back didn't hurry and feel better he was going to need a halfway house for TV addicts. Before she did anything else she was going to find those family group sheets.

12

*I*t was half an hour before the girls were due to come and Allison was a nervous wreck. It had been a dumb idea to have them come over to her house and she wished she had just called the bishop and quit. Not only was she nervous, she was exhausted. It had taken her all morning to get the house clean enough not to embarrass her, then all afternoon to make the frosting and tint it five different shades. She had wanted to make a cake for herself to decorate but she'd barely had time to mix up one for Sharon.

Now she was pushing Melinda around the house with her while she made one last check on things. She pushed Melinda up to the table that stood in the hall to collect everything as people came in the door. Tonight, however, it held only a family portrait, an African violet, and a frame holding her high school Honor Society certificate of membership. "I found it, Melinda," she said. She picked up the frame lovingly, holding it out for Melinda to see. "See, this means that Mommy used to be smart."

Sharon walked into the hall just then. "Oh, Mom. You're still smart. You've just been a mother for so long that nobody remembers."

Allison put the certificate down and smiled at Sharon. "Why, thank you, Sharon. That was real sweet to say." Then her stomach knotted again and she said, "Do you think everyone will like me, Sharon? I don't want anyone to quit because they don't want me to be the Young Women President."

"You'll do fine," Sharon said. She patted her mother on the shoulder. "No one ever likes the President at first anyway." She walked over to the front window and peeped out through the curtain. "I think someone is here now."

"Oh no," Allison said. "They're early." She turned Melinda around and started down the hall. "Where are Matthew and Mark?"

"They're in here," Brian said above the sound of the TV. "We're watching People's Court. I think Judge Wapner is going to really get these guys."

Allison took Melinda out of her wheelchair to lay her beside her daddy. "Brian, Melinda doesn't like this show. Here. I've got two Care-Bear books and her word cards. And here's her tape recorder and two tapes, and her musical teddy-bear."

"How long are you going to be gone?" Brian asked.

"I don't want her to get bored. And here are the boys' sticker books and the tinker toys and a box of vanilla wafers."

"We want to decorate cakes, Mommy," Mark said. "Can we come too?"

"You stay in here and you can come and see the cakes when they are finished," Allison said persuasively. "Okay?"

He stuck his lip out in a pout, which instantly made Allison feel guilty. This calling was already hurting her children.

"Come on, son," Brian said. "Let Mommy have her activity and then you can go out and see the cakes." He

rolled Melinda across him to put her between him and the
TV. "We'll have our own activity."

For some reason that idea appealed to Mark and he
jumped on the bed. "Can I give a talk, Daddy?"

Allison breathed a sigh of relief. Even when he was
hopelessly wasting his time, Brian was a great father.

"Look at that guy, Melinda," Brian said, pointing to the
TV. "He ran his golf-cart into that guy's garage door and
doesn't want to pay for the damages. I think the judge is
going to sock it to him." He tickled Melinda in the stomach
and she giggled. She loved her daddy. The boys started
socking each other.

"Brian!"

"We're fine, Allison. Go be a president."

The doorbell rang and the sound of giggling and
squealing filled the living room. That which she had feared
had obviously come to pass so she shut the door on Judge
Wapner, sighed a sigh of resignation, and crept down the
hall.

She had planned on standing on the fringes for a
couple of minutes to get a feel for the crowd but as soon as
she eased from the hall into the living room Terri Lynn saw
her and greeted her exuberantly. "Hi, Sister Lewis. Thanks
for letting us come to your house."

Then, just like an E. F. Hutton commercial, everyone
stopped talking and turned around to look at Allison. She
smiled a sincere, although shaky, smile. "We're glad to have
you." She didn't specify who the "we" included.

"Don't Terri Lynn and Rhonda look cute, Mom?"
Sharon asked. "They're cheerleaders. Terri Lynn's the
captain of the squad."

"Yes, they do, honey. Real nice." She sucked in her
stomach and straightened her shoulders. "All of you look
real nice." Nice? They all looked gorgeous. Thin, beautiful,
enthusiastic. She felt like Bert Parks at a Miss America
pageant.

"Is everyone here?" she asked.

"Everyone but Ashley," Rhonda said.

"Jared's bringing Ashley," Jennifer McCleary said sarcastically. She sighed and put her hand over her heart. "True love."

"You're just jealous," the cute blonde named Crystal said. "You wish some guy were bringing you."

Jennifer tossed her head and said, "Huh."

"Well, girls, would you like to go on into the kitchen and get started?" Allison asked. She was anxious to be in her kitchen where she reigned supreme. She might share the rest of the house with her family and even at this moment with all these girls but in her kitchen she was in her element. Others might fumble around looking for the mustard or wonder where she kept the chocolate chip cookies but she could put her hands on anything, at any time.

"Sure, let's go," Jennifer was saying. "It makes more sense than standing here holding these dumb cakes all night."

Okay, Jennifer, Allison thought. If you want to act like a three-year-old and ruin my first activity then I'll treat you like a three-year-old. "Would you like to help me put the bowls of frosting on the table, Jennifer?" she asked.

"I'd love to," Jennifer answered with a wry grin. Allison hadn't fooled her, but at least she knew that she hadn't fooled Allison, either, and that was fine with Allison. She was no fool.

"Let's see," Allison said after the opening prayer. She looked at all the girls now sitting around the kitchen table not saying anything. "Crystal? Erin? How about opening up all these bags of M&Ms and nuts and stuff and passing them around so everyone can get what they want?"

"Sure," they said. Allison was happy that they evidently weren't going to be a problem for her.

Maybe if she could just evaluate each girl individually she would wind up with just two problems — Jennifer and an infatuated Ashley.

"Where are your little boys?" Erin asked. "And Melinda?"

"They are so cute," Terri Lynn said. "Melinda has the prettiest smile."

"Thank you," Allison said. And then to Erin, "They are back with their Daddy. They don't fit in well with cake decorating."

"Oh, I'd help take care of them," she said almost apologetically.

"Erin loves to babysit," Sharon explained. "But I think one hour with Mark and Matthew would change her mind." Everyone laughed at that as Erin blushed.

The doorbell rang. "I'll get it," Sharon said. "It must be Ashley."

Allison jumped up quickly. "No, I'll get it." She put her hand on Sharon's shoulder to push her back down into her seat. Sharon looked surprised since Allison hadn't shared her plan to influence Ashley with her.

"Okay, Mom," Sharon said. "If it's that important to you, go get the door." She shrugged off Allison's grip. "Whatever makes you happy."

Allison backed out of the kitchen. "Get the knives and the spatulas, Sharon. They're on the counter."

It was Ashley and Jared at the door. They were standing on the porch, Jared tall and handsome in his gray letter jacket and Ashley small and sweet-looking. He was holding a plastic-wrapped cake in one arm and Ashley in the other, and she looked like she was exactly where she wanted to be.

Oh no, Allison thought. She liked them as a couple as soon as she saw them, not only because she was a hopeless romantic but because they looked like she and Brian used to look when he wore his high school letter jacket and she had his class ring around her neck. But as she thought this she also realized that Ashley's mother would not be pleased with the way her thoughts were running.

"Hi, come on in," she said. "You can come in, too, Jared, if you'd like." She took the cake from him and, as planned, put it beside the Honor Society certificate on the hall table.

"No. Thanks anyway, Sister Lewis," he said. "I need to get to church." He let Ashley go with reluctance and pinched her gently on the cheek. Allison knew it would have been a kiss if she hadn't been standing there. With a "See you later, good-looking" tossed over his shoulder he sprinted down the sidewalk.

Allison and Ashley watched him get into his car. "He's really cute," Allison said.

"I think so, too," Ashley said.

It was at this point that Allison had planned to pick up Ashley's cake and gently tap the Honor Society certificate with it. Then she was going to say, "Oh dear, I don't want to break this. Being in the Honor Society meant a lot to me when I was in high school."

But instead she picked up the cake without disturbing the certificate and said, "Here. Let's go in the kitchen and get started." Then she handed the cake to Ashley. When she had turned away, Allison put the frame face-down on the table.

"It was Ashley," she announced as they walked into the kitchen. All the girls were sitting down now with knives and cakes in front of them. The bowls of frosting were strategically placed in the center of the table but were untouched.

"Here's a seat for you, Ashley," Allison said.

"How's your love-life, Ashley?" Jennifer asked. She was sitting slouched down in her chair tapping her knife on the edge of a bowl.

Thinking fast to save herself from the irritating knife-tapping and Ashley from the inquisitive Jennifer, Allison said the first thing that came into her mind. "On your mark, get set, frost!"

It was silly but it worked. Everyone dipped their knives or spatulas into the nearest bowl of frosting and started spreading. It became quiet again, punctuated by groans and giggles as they dropped their frosting or tore a chunk out of their cakes. Allison worked her way around the table offering advice or smoothing out frosting with experienced hands. So far, so good, she thought.

As Jennifer explained to Allison that she could smooth out her frosting a lot better with the professional spatula her mother had, shouts of "Mommy, Mommy!" came from the bedroom.

"Excuse me, girls," Allison said. "I'll be right back."

She opened the bedroom door cautiously and caught Mark as he jumped out at her.

"Matthew wet his pants," Mark said.

"I couldn't get to him in time," Brian said sorrowfully. Then in a loud whisper, "How's it going out there?"

"I think they like me," she whispered back. "Except for Jennifer. She hates my spatula." She peeked into the bathroom where Matthew was standing in the bathtub holding his wet pants.

"Mark said stay," he said.

"What's wrong with your spatula?" Brian asked.

Allison swept out of the bedroom and was back with clean pajamas for Matthew in time to answer, "Who knows? I think she hates everything."

"Well, don't pay any attention to her," he said. "I like your spatula."

"Here." Allison plopped Matthew on the bed beside Brian. "Change him, please." She was out of the door before he could refuse.

Back in the kitchen everyone was about finished with their cakes. The person who caught Allison's eye first, though, was Mark who was sitting on Erin's lap licking frosting off a spoon.

She stopped in her tracks and put her hands on her hips. He must have escaped while she was getting the pajamas. "How did you get in here, Mark?" she asked.

He looked a little puzzled at her question then walked his fingers across the table and explained, "I walked."

"He's fine, Sister Lewis," Erin said. "I'll hold him."

Not sure that she wanted to risk a power struggle with a determined four-year-old when everything was going her way so far, Allison gave in without protest. If Matthew didn't escape too, maybe it would work out.

She felt a tug at her skirt as Crystal said, "He's so cute."

"Hello, Matthew," she said with resignation. She picked him up and gave him a squeeze since he was so cute in his clean pajamas and holding his teddy-bear.

"Here, I'll take him," Ashley said. "I love kids. I want to have a dozen." Jennifer and Sharon groaned.

Allison smiled and handed Matthew over. Matthew practically jumped into Ashley's lap when he saw her miniature marshmallows.

"I wanted twelve, too, when I was your age," Allison said. "Maybe I'll still make it."

"Mom!" Sharon shouted. "Don't depress me."

Allison pulled up a stool and decided that she was almost enjoying herself. If she could remember some of the get-acquainted games she had played at all the Tupperware parties she had been to, she would start one. It wouldn't hurt to know more about them if she was going to be spending so much time with them.

Ashley did it for her, though, when she suddenly asked, "How old were you when you got married, Sister Lewis?"

"Nineteen," Sharon said.

Allison thought a moment. "That seems awfully young now." She really meant it, too, even though she realized it was exactly what Ashley's mother would want her to say.

"Did your husband go on a mission?" Ashley asked.

"Yeah," Sharon answered. "To Germany. He even has some of those leather shorts and jacket that he wears on New Year's Eve when he's blowing this Bavarian hunter's horn at midnight."

"Really?" Jennifer said, not unkindly. "Doesn't he look kind of silly?"

"Actually yes," Allison said. "Now you know why we never host the ward New Year's Eve party."

Everyone laughed at that, so Allison took advantage of her popularity and said, "Why don't we go around the table and have everyone tell a little something about themselves so I can get to know you?"

Jennifer rolled her eyes and yawned in total boredom. Sharon caught her mother's eye and smiled a weak smile of support as Allison caught Jennifer's message.

Allison began to regret her decision until Terri Lynn enthusiastically said, "That's a great idea, Sister Lewis. If it's okay with everyone, I'll start."

"Go for it," Jennifer said.

Terri Lynn went for it. She started with what sketchy details she knew about her birth and went year by year, detail by detail through each year of her early childhood. By the time she reached her preschool years the other girls were beginning to whisper quietly to each other and Allison was trying to remember if this type of situation had ever occurred at a Tupperware party.

As Terri Lynn's trip down memory lane reached elementary school, Allison was relieved to hear Melinda screaming. She resisted the impulse to jump up, reassuring herself that Brian could handle this and that surely Terri Lynn wouldn't talk much longer.

She was wrong on both counts, though, because at the end of five minutes Terri Lynn was still going strong and Melinda was going stronger. It sounded like Melinda was about to enter another one of her screaming routines. "Excuse me," Allison said quietly, pointing to the bedroom.

Brian was holding Melinda on his stomach patting her on the back when Allison got there. "What's wrong with her?" she asked. She tried not to be irritated because she realized bedrest babysitting could not be too easy — but after all, this had been Brian's idea. Matthew and Mark were being good only because they were overdosing on M&Ms and marshmallows.

"I don't think you want to know," Brian said.

"I probably don't but tell me."

"She wants to go out with you," he said. "She looked around and wanted to know where Matthew and Mark were. When I told her they were out with you she said 'Me too'."

Allison put Melinda up on her shoulder and cupped her hand over her ear so Melinda couldn't hear what she whispered quietly to Brian. "If I take her out she'll just want to eat all the junk the boys are eating and I can't feed her and help the girls with their cakes."

"Okay," he said. "I'll do my best."

Melinda quieted down a little so Allison held her back in her arms and said, "Mommy's real busy out in the kitchen. If you stay in here a little bit with Daddy I'll come and get you when the cakes are finished and you can see pretty cakes. Okay?"

Melinda shook her head vigorously and said, "No."

Brian held out his arms to take Melinda back. "Just go on, Allison. She'll be okay after a while. Bring us some M&Ms or something." Melinda didn't agree with his assessment of the situation. She shook her head again, but Brian took her anyway as Allison leaned down. He said reassuringly, "Go on. I can handle it."

Allison walked on over to the door but when she looked back at Melinda's sad face she couldn't stand it. It wasn't Melinda's fault she couldn't hold a spoonful of frosting by herself. Allison hated situations like this, but she knew she couldn't break the heart of this little girl who just wanted to be a part of whatever fun was causing so much laughter in the kitchen.

"All right," she said. "If Mommy takes you out in the kitchen in your wheelchair will you sit there like a nice little girl and watch? Mommy won't be able to hold you like she usually does."

Melinda's big smile returned immediately as she nodded her head. Brian wiped her tears away with the sheet. "You be a good girl for Daddy, okay?"

Allison put her in her wheelchair and pushed her over to the dresser to brush her hair. Melinda was all smiles. It took so little to make her happy that Allison felt like a jerk for not wanting to take her out. But please, she prayed silently, let her be happy to just sit and watch this time.

Brian was already wrapped up in the covers staring at "Jeopardy" by the time she reached the door. When he turned over to remind her to turn the lights off before she left she suddenly felt less like saintly Florence Nightingale administering to the sick and more like a wife soon to be irritated.

"Brian," she said precisely. "I may be mistaken but I believe you got the better end of this deal."

"What can I say?" he said. "I tried."

He had, she guessed, softening just a bit. "But that doesn't change the fact that I'm now taking care of all the children *you* were supposed to take care of."

He just muttered something inaudible under the covers and the softening process stopped as the irritation welled up again. She snapped the light off with as much anger as her finger could muster. They would talk later.

"Someone else to join us," she announced coming through the kitchen door. She pushed Melinda over as close to Terri Lynn and Rhonda as the wheelchair and her barstool would fit since she already knew they were nice to little girls in wheelchairs.

"We finished the game, Sister Lewis," Erin said.

"Once we got Terri Lynn done it didn't take long for the rest of us," Jennifer said.

"You finished?" Allison said with disappointment. So much for the rest of the story.

It wasn't long before everyone's cake was lined up on the table smoothly iced and decorated. Allison felt as proud as Sara Lee. For some reason, all her children had behaved and all the girls, except Jennifer, seemed to like her. Erin was great with Matthew and Mark, letting them cover her whole cake with M&Ms. She was going to encourage Sharon to have Erin over a lot in the future to spend the night.

"I want to buy my cake at the auction," Mark said, pointing to the M&M cake.

"I do too," Allison said. "I bet it wins the prize for the most colorful."

"Or the sweetest," Erin said.

Allison remembered just then that she had a surprise for the girls. That afternoon she had mixed up some lemonade and dusted off the popcorn popper to surprise the girls with refreshments if the evening had gone well. She had not told Sharon in case none of the girls liked her and she didn't like any of them. In that case she had planned to send them home quickly without refreshments.

In her opinion, though, they deserved refreshments. She opened the refrigerator to get out the lemonade but stopped and listened when she thought she heard a desperate cry of "Allison, Allison" coming from down the hall. It was Brian.

"Be right back, girls," she said. Slamming the refrigerator door, she once again raced down the hall.

She reached his side in record time and grabbed his shoulder. "What's wrong, honey?"

"Quick," he said. "It's Final Jeopardy. Who was the last American president to be elected but not appoint a Supreme Court Justice during his term? I'm tied with the champion but I don't know this answer."

"What?" she said. She could hardly believe what he was saying but when she followed his gaze to the TV she saw indeed it was the Final Jeopardy part of Jeopardy.

"I don't know and I don't care," she said. "And what's more I'm going to turn the TV off." And she did. It took bravery and courage, but she snapped it off. "And what's more," she said, "if you don't read or do something else I'm going to put the TV in the hall and you won't even be able to crawl and get it." She picked up the nearest magazine and threw it at him. "Here. Read it."

Something she said must have impressed him. "Okay, okay," he said. "It's just a game show. No need to get so upset." He flipped open the Ladies Home Journal she had so gently given him. "I'll read, I'll read."

"Now. I'm going back out and finish my cake decorating and I don't want to hear another word from this room," she said in her sternest voice.

He just ignored her and stared at the calcium supplement ad he was reading. She glared at him a few seconds but he kept reading. When she heard the doorbell ring she left and walked down the hall for what seemed to be the twentieth time that evening. Not wanting the little incident with Brian to be blown out of proportion, she decided to bring some popcorn and lemonade back to him.

When she got to the end of the hall, though, most of the girls were in the living room putting their coats on. Even Jared was back, helping Ashley on with her coat. Terri Lynn's father was there jiggling his car keys impatiently.

"You girls aren't leaving already, are you?" Allison asked. It really seemed to her that they had just begun.

"Mom, it's eight o'clock," Sharon said. "That's what time it ends."

"But I was going to fix some refreshments," she said.

"That's real nice, Sister Lewis," Terri Lynn said. "We're all on diets anyway. But thanks for having us over."

"You're welcome," Allison answered, following them to the front door. She actually wanted to scream "Thank you, thank you for being nice to me" — except Jennifer, of course — but she thought she should retain some dignity in front of Brother Parker. She chose instead to wave cheerfully and casually call out "I'll see you Friday" as they all walked down the sidewalk.

Jared and Ashley lingered on the porch a little, waiting until the others were out of earshot to turn back to Allison. Oh no, Allison thought. She was too tired to hear confessions or share awful secrets tonight.

"I don't know how to say this, Sister Lewis," Ashley began.

"Don't say anything if you don't want to," Allison said.

"No, I need to," Ashley said. Allison held her breath. "My mother might be calling you sometime. I found out she used to call Sister Spence."

Allison let her breath out slowly. "Your mother?" she asked with just the right amount of surprise in her voice.

"She's sort of flipped her lid," Jared said. "She thinks we're going to elope or something."

"I just wanted you to know," Ashley said. Then she confessed, "I got really mad when I found out. It's sort of …" She hesitated.

Jared finished for her. "Embarrassing."

"Well, thanks for telling me," Allison said. "But I don't have anything to tell her, do I?" Her mind raced as she said that, but the only thing she remembered Ashley saying about marriage was about Brian's and Allison's marriage and she was sure that didn't count.

Then she found herself making the Offer — the one that could only lead to trouble. She didn't really want to say it, but since she knew what a tremendous responsibility she had as a teacher she said it anyway. "Just remember if you kids ever need to talk to someone I'm here."

"Thanks a lot, Sister Lewis," Ashley said. "We'll remember."

And then they were gone as Allison stood on the porch hoping against all hope that Ashley's mother wouldn't call in the morning and that they never needed to talk to her.

A while later Allison stood outside the bedroom door, dreading to go in to Brian. Usually she tried to get the children in bed as quickly as possible but tonight she had lingered over the routine, picking up stray socks, bringing everyone a glass of water they hadn't asked for, even reading a bedtime story. Matthew finally fell asleep halfway through the story and Mark had asked at the end if she could skip the next story because he had had a long day and needed some rest. But now it was time to go in to Brian and see if he was mad at her for fussing at him. She could hear the TV going so he couldn't have taken her too seriously.

She opened the door slowly, hoping he had fallen asleep. When she peeked her head in, though, as quietly as she could, she saw that he was over on his side with his back to the TV, reading the Wall Street Journal. The next thing she noticed was the white washcloth tied to the TV antenna.

He looked up and she came in, smiled, and said, "I surrender."

"Are you mad at me?" she asked.

"Nope. Are you mad at me?"

"Nope." She kicked off her shoes and laid down next to his newspaper.

"Did the kids give you any trouble?" he asked.

"Nope."

"Why?"

"Her name is Erin and she loves our children."

"Can we adopt her?"

"She even fed Melinda marshmallows when I was back here with you." Most people were too afraid to feed Melinda anything.

"So they liked you?" he said.

"I think so. The vote's still out on Jennifer, but I think the others liked me. And they want to come over New Year's Eve to see you in your little leather shorts."

He groaned. "You told them?"

She smiled and nodded her head. Then she yawned a huge yawn. "Tonight went okay but if I have to work this hard every week I'll die of old age. She picked up her bathrobe. "I'm going to take a shower."

"If you hurry you can catch the beginning of a good movie that starts in a couple of minutes," he said.

"Brian!"

"So, we'll call it a date."

"Okay," she said. The way she felt she'd only be awake a couple of minutes anyway. She dragged herself over to the bathroom but right before she shut the door she said, "By the way, it was Jimmy Carter."

"*Who* was Jimmy Carter?"

"The last elected president not to appoint any Supreme Court justices during his administration."

"Are you sure?" he said.

"Of course I'm sure," she said confidently. "I was a member of the Honor Society. Remember?"

As she went into the bathroom he buried his face in his hands and muttered something about ten thousand dollars.

13

"I'm taking the day off," Allison said to Brian. She had just come in from taking Melinda out to her mini-bus.

"You are?" he said. He was finishing up his breakfast of peanut butter toast and apple juice which was the best she could offer until she could get back to the grocery store.

"It's Mother's Day Out at the Y," she said. "And I'm a mother, this is the day, and I'm going out." She picked up the candy wrappers and newspapers that had accumulated around Brian's little corner of the bed since the afternoon before. "I haven't been out for a while, you know."

On the Thursday mornings she took advantage of the preschool program at the YWCA. She rushed through her housework in thirty minutes flat, threw some clothes on the boys, and threw them in the car to be at the Y by nine o'clock. That gave her three and a half hours to herself. Sometimes she swam for a little before she left the Y, sometimes she went to the library and buried herself in a spy novel, and sometimes she went to the mall and ate too much chocolate at the chocolate store.

"Who will take care of me?" he asked. He looked up at her with almost sad eyes. She had noticed that the longer he stayed flat on his back in pajamas the more he had become dependent on her. It hadn't really bothered her yet since under normal circumstances she spent most of her time taking care of her family anyway. But today she needed to get out for awhile and he needed to understand that. She would try to be gentle.

She stopped picking up clothes and sat down on the bed beside him. "Brian. Darling," she said. "I have spent more time in the house this week than I have in ages. Now, I don't mind because I want you to get well, but I really need to have some time to myself this morning or I might go crazy." She patted him reassuringly on the arm. "I've packed your lunch and I'll bring it in before I go. And I won't be gone long so please don't mind me going."

Her eyes pleaded with him to understand as she waited expectantly for his answer.

He looked at her intently for a few seconds, then he smiled and pulled her down beside him in a big hug. "You're right," he said. "I guess I've gotten a little spoiled this week."

"You said it, not me," she said, her voice muffled against his shoulder. "I'll be back by one."

He pushed her up again, then kissed her. "There's a Clint Eastwood movie on this morning anyway."

"I'm glad I'm going then," she said. She picked up her makeup bag and went into the bathroom.

"If you feel like it when you get home," he said, "you can help me with my family group sheets."

"Be glad to," she said, powdering her nose. Maybe she could forgive him for the Clint Eastwood movie and all the rest of the TV he would watch this morning if they spent some time together this afternoon working on genealogy. After all, you were supposed to have some balance in your life.

*

She was as good as her word — she and the boys were home at twelve forty-five. She had had a wonderful morning, quiet and alone, and felt refreshed. "Go see if Daddy's okay," she said. She dropped the mail on the hall table, checking in the mirror to see if her hair still looked nice. It did, so she went right back to the bedroom where the boys had jumped on the bed and were telling their daddy excitedly what they had done all morning at their school.

Brian was studying a popsicle giraffe and penguin when she walked in. "Wowee," he said. "Boys, what did you let Mommy do to herself? Doesn't she look pretty?"

"She cut all her curls off," Mark said. "And she didn't even save them in a baggie like she did with Matthew's."

"Do you like it?" Allison said, twirling around in a high fashion pirouette. I decided to try the new sleek, smooth look."

"It's beautiful, honey. Did you do anything else extravagant?"

"I bought a new dress," she said. She pulled a pretty pink and gray striped dress out of the bag.

"You did?" he asked. He really meant "How much?"

"It was on sale," she assured him.

"I didn't ask," he said. He reached for the other bag but she grabbed it away from him.

"Nothing interesting," she said quickly. She put the bag out of his reach on the dresser. "I guess I'll get the boys to bed."

"So what's in the bag?" he yelled as she walked out.

"Surprises, surprises," she yelled back. And it was going to be a great surprise, she hoped. When she was at the grocery store she was reminded of all the naked cakes she had helped cover the night before and an idea was born. If all the girls and other women could decorate a cake for the cake auction why couldn't she? She had only thought about helping the Young Women with their cakes and hadn't even considered one for herself. But if she baked it after the children were in bed tonight and decorated it tomorrow during naptime she could have a wonderful surprise. So she'd bought a cake mix.

She stuck it high up in a cupboard and dumped all the decorating tips and attachments she'd bought into a drawer. She wasn't even going to tell anyone until it was finished and beautiful. Roses used to be her specialty so she was going to cover the cake with delicate roses and thin little leaves. If she took her time and was very careful she was sure she could win the most beautiful cake prize or even the best overall. Brian would be proud of her and all the Young Women, including Jennifer, might get the idea that she actually knew something worth learning.

She started to put the other groceries away, but a banging followed by an "Oh no" coming from the boys' room changed her priorities. She headed in the direction of the possible disaster much against her will.

"What was that all about?" Brian asked her a few minutes later. She had just collapsed on the bed beside him, shaking her head.

"Those boys of yours," she said.

"If I have to claim them it must have been something terrible."

"It involved a Nerf ball, vaseline, and a bent curtain rod." She heard familiar voices on the TV and realized that she had missed almost fifteen minutes of "Days of Our Lives." She glanced over at Brian, who was busy straightening up family group sheets and pencils. She had forgotten about their genealogy date and was not thrilled about remembering it.

But Brian didn't say a thing. In fact, he didn't say a thing until she was deeply involved in a scene with Bo, and Hope discussing Bo's reluctance to share the secrets of his past life in the merchant marine. Then he said, "I can't figure out Hope Brady's relationship with Alice Horton."

"Granddaughter," Allison said.

"So who's her father?" he asked.

"Doug," she said. "He and Julie live in Switzerland where Doug is recovering from several heart attacks. Every time something happens that they should be at, Doug has another stupid heart attack. They didn't even make it to Bo's and Hope's wedding. The queen of England came, though."

"So Hope's mother is Julie?" he asked.

"No, it's Addie — Julie's mother."

"What? Run that one by me again," he said.

"Doug was married to Addie, Tom and Alice's daughter, years ago. Addie had been married before and had a daughter named Julie. So Julie was Doug's stepdaughter, no blood relation. Remember that, it's important. Then Addie and Doug had Hope which made her Alice's granddaughter. Then Addie died and Doug fell in love with Julie, his stepdaughter and Hope's half-sister. Hope never did like Julie too much after that."

Brian was quiet a minute, then asked, "So Doug and Julie and Doug and Addie would need separate group sheets?"

It took a second for his question to make any sense to her. When it finally dawned on her just whose genealogy information he was recording she jerked around to face him. "Brian, you aren't putting the Hortons on all these sheets are you?"

"No," he said. "I have one for the Bradys, the DiMeras, and Neil and Liz Somebody."

"Why?" she said. "You can't do their temple work, honey. This is a TV show, or have you forgotten that?"

"I haven't forgotten," he said defensively. "I just wanted to make it easier for you to know what's going on." He smiled at her as she stared unbelievingly. "I've started on 'Another World', too," he offered.

She finally thought of something to say. "Don't even tell me about it," she said. "Eternities from now when I have to stand and account for the things I've learned on this earth I don't want to know anything about this. You can explain it."

"Here," he said. He handed her the stack of papers. "I did it for you. Just because I love you."

She took them from him because she thought he might have gone just a little crazy being penned up for so long and maybe she should humor him.

She stood up and turned off the TV, still holding onto his present. "You take a nap, Brian. You need some rest." She closed the drapes and took the pencil from his hand. At first she laid it on the dresser but then changed her mind and took it with her. It had a dangerously sharp point.

"This is nothing to get upset about, Allison," he protested.

"I know it isn't, darling," she said. "Just don't worry about it. Just stay calm and get some rest."

"But...but I just wanted to help," he sputtered as she closed the door quietly behind her.

She tiptoed into the family room and turned the TV on. She knew he was still basically mentally sound, but being in that one room for so long had temporarily misadjusted his priorities. A couple more days, though, and his back would be well and he could get some fresh air and she'd get her old Brian back. In the meantime she'd just have to hold the family together.

She glanced over the group sheets in her hands. How he had been able to unravel some of the tangled relationships he had recorded was a mystery to her. She would like to think that it had been therapeutic for him. At least it had focused his mind on something other than pain for a while.

Oh okay, she thought as a wave of tenderness for him swept over her. I'll play his game until he is well.

She picked up the Brady family sheets and shook her head. That one wasn't quite perfect, but she couldn't blame him, since he had no way of knowing that Roman, Bo, and Kimberly had a sister named Kayla who had left the show last summer. So just because she loved Brian she filled in Kayla's name for him. On the bottom line, since she was the baby of the family.

14

*A*s it turned out, Allison didn't bake her cake after the children went to bed because she wore herself out entertaining the children and keeping them in the family room while a bishopric meeting was held in the bedroom. She hadn't told Brian but she had called the bishop and suggested another bedside bishopric meeting. Brian needed some male companionship more than she needed the cake baked.

So the next morning she baked it hurriedly while the boys were outside playing and laid the layers out to cool on the dining room table where they only ate when they had company. She sprayed Lysol all over the house to mask the aroma as it baked.

"Brian," she said through the bathroom door where he was shaving. "I'm going to go outside to cut some flowers for the cake auction tonight. I won't be outside long."

He opened the door and asked through a faceful of shaving cream, "Are you going to that tonight?"

"That's what I bought the dress for," she said.

"Are you going to take all the kids?"

"I have to," she said. "I'm not making any more babysitting deals with you."

"I'll be all by myself?"

"It won't be for long," she assured him. "And it will be during Wheel of Fortune and Jeopardy so you'll have something to do. You can put Vanna White and Pat Sajak on a pedigree chart or something."

"Don't be sarcastic," he said lightly. Then he added with a wink, "Thanks for correcting my charts."

She grabbed the doorknob to the bathroom door, closing it quickly and almost smashing his face. "I don't want to talk about it."

He opened the door again. "Do you want to hear some great news?"

"It depends."

"My back feels much better."

"It does?"

"Look — I can even move around a little." He put his hands on his waist and twisted his shoulders. "I think another day in bed and I'll be okay."

She looked doubtful. "I think maybe a weekend in bed — a long one. You don't want to take it too fast."

"Yes sir, Dr. Lewis." He saluted her. "My face is drying out. Give me a kiss before you go." He puckered up.

She shut the door in his face again and went outside to cut chrysanthemums. The boys came running to her when she rounded the house.

"Did you come outside to play with us, Mommy?" Mark asked. They were both covered with sand.

"I came out to cut some flowers to take to church tonight," she told them.

"Can we buy our M&M cake?" he asked.

"Do you have any money?" she asked, smiling at them.

Mark thought a little, then his face brightened. "I'll go loan some from Daddy."

"Good luck," she said. "Loan some for me, too."

"Okay," he said. He turned to run away.

"Don't go in the house with all that sand on you," she said. "Come here and I'll brush you off. You too, Matthew." Matthew had been standing nearby wiggling and jumping up and down, so she added, "Take Matthew into the bathroom when you go in."

They ran off and she began to survey her flower bed. A few straggly zinnias and chrysanthemums were about all that was left of her late fall assortment, so she started in on them. She was almost finished when the back door opened and Mark yelled out, "Can I fix Daddy a snack? He wants something exciting."

Remembering the bologna and graham crackers of the other day she said, "Yes, but don't make a mess." Poor Brian, she thought. Maybe she should go help Mark in his selection. At that moment she froze. Right in the middle of the zinnias. She tried to assure herself that there was no logical reason that Mark would go into the dining room and find her cake on the table and feed it to Brian. She didn't convince herself, though, and got slowly to her feet, trying to stay calm. Ignoring the desire to run, she walked deliberately around the house and into the front door. She didn't even stop to put her flowers in water, but walked straight back to the bedroom.

When she got there and saw the three of them on the bed munching huge handfuls of cake she groaned and dropped her head against the doorframe.

"Great cake, honey," Brian said. "Did you mean to frost it?"

She was too upset to even trust herself to go in and fuss with them. She walked slowly into the kitchen and tossed her bouquet into the sink then, squaring her shoulders, she walked into the dining room to assess the damage.

Mark had cut it neatly — not making a mess just like she had told him. One of these days she would compliment him on that point. And he had been fair. Each layer had a pie-shaped piece of the same size cut from it.

She sat down at the table, shoulders now drooping, and stared at the cake. Someone bumped against her chair. It was Mark and he looked scared. "Daddy says you're mad at me," he said.

"I'm not very happy, Mark," she said. "I was going to decorate the cake for tonight."

"I'm sorry," he said. His chin started quivering as his eyes filled up with tears. "You said I could fix him a snack."

She put her arm around him. "I know I did," she said. "But I just didn't think you would come out here and cut the cake." She hugged him as all the church commercials about forgiving and listening passed through her mind. Then she held him back and looked him in the eyes. "Okay, we'll have a new rule. From now on if anything is in the dining room it is not to be eaten. Agreed?"

"Agreed," he said. He looked over the cake sadly, but then his face lit up. "I made it look like Pac-Man, Mommy. Make a Pac-Man." He looked over at her hopefully and promised, "I'll buy it."

"That's okay, honey," she said. She got up from the table and considered the cake again. "You're right — it does look like Pac-Man." Putting her arm around Mark, she decided to be brave and inventive. "Okay, let's go get the yellow food coloring and make a Pac-Man cake." She could still win best-tasting or most original.

They started out to the kitchen, friends again. But before they got very far they heard Brian yelling, "Matthew's throwing up!"

Allison grabbed Mark's hand and they raced down the hall. Some day, she thought, some day when the kids are all grown I'll miss all this excitement. Some day.

15

"So let me see your cake before you go," Brian said. He was lying in bed watching her put her makeup on again. Matthew was curled up beside him with his blanket and teddy-bear.

"It's just your everyday Pac-Man cake," she said.

"I've never seen one before," he said.

"Well — ." She put her lipstick on. "If you promise not to laugh I'll bring it back."

"Why would I laugh?" he said. "I think it's a cute idea. I bet you win the most creative cake award."

"Maybe so," she said noncommittally. She hadn't told anyone that she really wanted to win an award in case she didn't. "I'll go get it."

She left and returned a few minutes later with a Pac-Man cake. Since there was not a whole lot you could do to mess up a cake that required only one plain round eye, it was a perfect Pac-Man cake.

"I think it's cute, honey," Brian said.

She looked at him dubiously, then down at the cake. "Well, at least we know it tastes good. Don't we?"

"It's delicious," he agreed.

She put the cake on the dresser and went over to sit by Matthew on the bed. Putting her hand on his forehead, she said, "I don't think he has a fever so I'm sure he'll be all right. Just an upset tummy, I bet." She bent down and kissed him on the forehead. "Will you be all right with Daddy?"

He yawned widely and nodded his head.

"Are you sure you can take care of him?" she asked Brian.

"Yes, don't worry," he said. "He's almost asleep now." He covered Matthew's shoulders up with his blanket. "We'll be fine."

"Don't try to put him to bed," she said. "You shouldn't lift him so just leave him here and I'll put him to bed when we get home."

"Yes, Mother," Brian said. "Now give me a kiss and go." He glanced over at the TV before he puckered up.

"I know," she said. "It's time for People's Court." She leaned over and kissed him. "Good-bye and call me if you need me. Do you know the number at church?"

"I'm in the bishopric, remember?"

"That means that other people call *you* there."

"Yes, Mother, I know the number" he said. "Now go."

Andrew guarded Pac-Man in the car on the way to church while Sharon fussed and wished that her cake was as pretty as Terri Lynn's.

"Yours is real pretty, Sharon, so just stop worrying," Allison said, turning into the parking lot. In fact, she had considered offering Sharon five dollars to trade cakes with her but had decided instead to hold her head high and be content with whichever ribbon the judges wanted her to have. Best-tasting would be fine with her.

The first person Allison saw as she pushed Melinda into the foyer was Ashley's mother, Liz. Her heart sank. She hadn't given much thought to Liz since Ashley had left

Wednesday night. Now she wished she had planned what she was going to say to her the next time they spoke. Hi, I think Ashley and Jared are a perfect match. No, that wouldn't work. Don't worry, Liz, our next lesson is on college, chastity, and the contribution single sisters can make to the church. That might work.

What she decided to do was to look hurried and walk quickly by her with a casual "hi." She almost made it to the social hall — until Liz grabbed her arm and said, "I'm glad you came, Allison."

"Thank you," Allison said, stopping.

"Can we talk?" Liz asked. Her grip on Allison's arm tightened.

"I need to go register my cake," Allison said. "We're a little late." Liz didn't let go.

Allison looked down at Andrew who was waiting patiently with the cake. Then she sighed. If she didn't talk to Liz her arm was going to have to be amputated. "Andrew, why don't you go register my cake?"

"Sharon will help you. Won't you, Sharon?" Liz said. She dragged Allison over to a corner of the foyer before she finally let go of her arm. "What do you think about Ashley and Jared?" she demanded.

"I think they are both very nice," Allison said carefully.

"I don't mean that," Liz said. "I mean do you think they are going to elope or anything? Do you think they have — you know?"

"You mean — ?" Allison asked shocked.

"Yes. Do you?"

"No," Allison said emphatically. "I think that they are very nice, well-behaved kids and I really think you are getting too upset." She said it kindly, trying to inch away. "I know you can trust Ashley. Really." How was she going to get away from this wild-eyed woman?

Liz grabbed her arm again. "Do you really think so? I mean really?"

Allison looked over toward the social hall where most of the people were sitting down. She didn't see any of her children and could only hope that Andrew had registered her cake. Turning back to Liz, she patted the hand that clenched her arm. "Liz, please try to calm down. Maybe if you had a talk with Ashley and Jared you'd feel better."

"I have," she said. "But they say they love each other."

Allison knew she was treading on thin ice here. "Maybe they do, Liz. In their own way, of course." Allison had no idea what that meant, but it sounded good. "But I'm sure they'll be fine."

Liz looked like she wanted to believe her.

Just then, thankfully, Sharon walked over. "Mom, come on. It's starting."

"Okay, honey, I'm coming." She looked back at Liz. "I promise I'll have a talk with Ashley and make sure everything is okay."

"Thank you, Allison," Liz said. "I appreciate it."

Allison smiled at her. "Sure," she said. "Now, come on Melinda, let's go buy a cake."

She pulled Melinda's brake off and quickly wheeled her into the social hall where Andrew and Sharon had saved them a seat in one of the back rows. "What do you think of the competition?" she whispered to Sharon. She sat down and pulled Melinda close to her.

"There are some really pretty cakes, Mom," she answered. "I don't know if we can win or not."

"But there are no more Pac-man cakes, Mom," Andrew said.

The auction was going to be first with the judges looking over and tasting the cakes while everyone was bidding. Each family had been given a number to hold up to bid on the cakes.

The first two cakes went for ten dollars each which was the amount Allison had decided she could spend on one. But she didn't know whether to spend it on hers, Sharon's, or the M&M cake. She didn't want any of the other girls mad at her if she bought Erin's.

Allison looked down at Melinda who was not going to be happy for very long sitting on the back row looking at everybody's back. "Do you want to sit on Mommy's lap?" she asked Melinda. Maybe she could hold her up high enough for her to see the cakes. She missed Brian; he was always the one who kept Melinda happy when they went anyplace.

As she reached down to get Melinda, who had turned instantly happy, Mark began jumping up and down on his chair and hitting her on the shoulder. "Mommy, Mommy, there's my M&M cake!" he shouted.

"Okay," she whispered. "Now be quiet." She finished unbuckling Melinda and lifted her out of her wheelchair, dropping her diaper and coat in the process. "Oh great," she groaned.

"Mommy, Mommy, my cake," Mark kept shouting.

"Mom, Mom," Sharon whispered loudly. Then, "Mark, Mark, no."

"Just a minute," Allison said from the floor. With Melinda dangling off the side of her lap she was fumbling around on the floor for the coat and diaper. She was getting very irritated.

As she found them and straightened back up she saw Sharon reach over and grab Mark, dragging him across Andrew's lap onto hers.

"Where's our number, Sharon?" Allison asked. Before Sharon could answer her Allison heard the auctioneer bang his gavel and announce, "Sold for sixteen dollars to the lucky family with the number twenty-one!"

"Oh no," Allison said. She had missed out and she loved M&Ms. But how was she supposed to bid on anything when she didn't even have the stupid number. "Where's the stupid number?" she whispered across to Sharon who was wrestling something out of Mark's hand.

When Sharon had wrenched whatever it was in his hand away from him she handed it over to her mother. "Here, Mom. It's the lucky number twenty-one that just bought the cake for sixteen dollars."

*

The rest of the auction Mark was held prisoner in Sharon's lap as Andrew sat on the lucky number twenty-one. It was hard for Allison to hold Melinda up high enough to see the cakes because she was so tight and her balance was so poor. Allison finally stood up in the back and held Melinda out in front of her.

It seemed to take forever for the judges to start putting ribbons behind the cakes. Allison finally sat down and put Melinda back in her wheelchair because her arms were aching.

"I'm going to push Melinda out into the foyer and stand at the other door," she whispered to Sharon.

The foyer was empty but the door closest to the cake table was crowded with several of the brothers. As Allison stood behind them on tiptoes and strained to see over she heard an excited little boy's voice behind her. She turned to see Mark and Sharon running across the foyer to her.

"Mommy, Mommy, you got a ribbon," Mark was screaming.

"I did?" she asked.

Sharon reached her and said, "You got a ribbon, Mom. I couldn't see which one but I saw them put a ribbon behind your cake."

Allison was excited. She looked down at Melinda who was straining to see what was going on behind her. "Mommy got a ribbon," Allison said to her. She patted her on the shoulder as Melinda broke into a wide smile.

"Let's go in, Mom," Sharon said. She motioned to the crowded door.

"We can't go through there," Allison said.

"They'll let the wheelchair through," Sharon said. "People always move for it."

Allison knew that was true. It was one of the two or three advantages of having a child in a wheelchair she had been able to find.

"Well, okay," she said. "But hold onto Mark and don't push."

The brothers parted faster than the Red Sea when Allison politely said, "Excuse me." Allison and her brood slipped through and flattened themselves against the wall near one end of the table. The announcer was at the other end, just beginning to announce the prizes. The judge handed each ribbon separately to the announcer and held up the award-winning cake as he read the ribbon. Allison's was about halfway down the table.

When the judge picked up Sharon's cake and the ribbon behind it, Sharon was thrilled and grabbed Allison's arm. Her poor bruised arm. Allison gritted her teeth and held Sharon's hand as the judge announced, "Most colorful cake ribbon to Sharon Lewis." Sharon stopped jumping and let go of Allison's arm.

"Most colorful," she said with disgust. "That's a stupid ribbon."

"Oh it is not," Allison said. "It means it's a pretty cake. Go get your ribbon."

Sharon frowned, hesitating as the judge searched for the winner of the ribbon he was holding up. She poked Mark in the back and ordered, "Go get the ribbon, Mark."

He took off running and screeched to a halt in front of the judge. "That's my sister's," he said.

Sharon buried her head on Allison's shoulder. "I'm going to kill him."

Allison watched with interest as the judges got closer and closer to her cake. The most beautiful had already been awarded but she could handle that. Sister Murphy had won the ribbon for the most unusual and since the cake was yellow Allison was sure it had squash in it somehow.

The judges passed over Terri Lynn's cake, which made Sharon feel better. Pac-Man was next.

She tried to look surprised and humble as the judge held up her cake. A few chuckles broke out in the audience but she could handle that. After all, it had won a ribbon.

"Look at this Pac-Man, kids," the announcer said. "Isn't it great?" He looked down at the ribbon in his hand. Allison thought the pause was a nice dramatic touch. He continued. "This Pac-Man has won himself a ribbon for the ..." He paused again. "The funniest cake here tonight."

Allison was mortified. She could not remember the last time she had been so embarrassed. She had the presence of mind somehow, though, to keep her humble smile pasted on her lips and poke Mark in the back. "Go get it, Mark."

He took off again. "That's my Mommy!" he shouted this time. Everyone laughed and looked over to where Allison was trying to sink behind the wheelchair.

"Do you like Pac-Man?" the announcer asked. To Allison it seemed like he was taking advantage of her humiliation.

"I helped make him," he said. Then he demonstrated with two karate chops to the table precisely how he had helped.

"Don't worry, Mom," Sharon whispered to Allison. Putting her arm around her mother's shoulder she said, "I'll strangle him for both of us."

Allison had planned a fast get-away after the last cake was auctioned but so many people were at the table picking up cakes that she had to speak with some of them.

"Sister Lewis," Sister McFarren said. "Your Pac-Man cake was so sweet! Will you make me one for my grandson's birthday? He would just love it!"

"When's his birthday?" Allison asked, hoping he had just had one.

"He just had one a couple of weeks ago, so it will be quite a while," she answered.

"Sure," Allison said. "Remind me a few weeks in advance." Surely she'll forget.

Sister McFarren shook her head and patted Allison's arm. "Sister Lewis, you are so special."

A crowd of girls rushed up and surrounded Allison. "Sister Lewis," Terri Lynn said. "That's so neat, you winning the funniest ribbon. Your cake was so-o-o cute." Allison smiled weakly. "Thanks."

"You didn't tell us that's what you were going to do," Erin said. "We probably would have stolen your idea." "Oh, don't say that," Allison said. "All of your cakes were beautiful."

"I made the Pac-Man," Mark said proudly.

"You did?" Erin asked.

Allison pulled him back against her and cupped his chin in her hand. It was easy access to cover his mouth.

"Did you see who got your cake, Erin?" Allison asked.

"I did, I did," Mark mumbled from behind his mother's hand.

"You got our cake?" Erin asked him.

He nodded vigorously.

"Would you like to take him to get it?" Allison asked.

"Sure. Come on," Erin said. They left, Mark jumping up and down in excitement.

Allison bent down to put Melinda's coat on. She continued to smile as she whispered out of the corner of her mouth, "Sharon, if you ever tell anyone about my cake I will never clean up the kitchen again. You will."

Sharon whispered back out of the corner of her mouth. "Sounds like a deal to me. In fact, you take Melinda out to the car and I'll bring the boys out." She crossed her heart.

Allison wasted no time in getting out the door.

16

*W*hen she and Melinda reached the parking lot the first people Allison saw were Ashley and Jared. They were standing beside Jared's car which, of course, was parked right next to Allison's car. She stopped before they could see her but there was really no way to avoid seeing them unless she waited for them to leave, and the air was too chilly to keep Melinda out for very long.

Okay, she thought, it must be meant to be. She pushed on, reaching her car as Ashley and Jared turned around and saw her. "Hi," she said. "Did you enjoy the auction?"

"Yes," Ashley said. "Jared bought my cake." She smiled up at him. "I knew he would, though, because I made his favorite kind. I hope my mother is going to let him take me home and have a piece."

"Oh," Allison said. But then she had to say something more inspiring to them than that since she had promised Liz she would. But what?

"It's awfully chilly out here," she finally said. "You should be inside where it's warm." And there are other people to watch you.

It was the wrong thing to say. Ashley moved closer to Jared for warmth and he put his arm around her. Allison began putting Melinda in the car.

"Here, I'll help you with the wheelchair, Sister Lewis," Jared said. He untangled himself from Ashley and reached for the wheelchair.

"Is Brother Lewis feeling better?" Ashley asked.

"A little bit," Allison answered, closing the car door. "It will be nice to have him up and around again." Go on, Allison, go on, she urged herself. "Marriage can really be trying sometimes."

"Oh, I'd love to take care of Jared if anything ever happened to him," Ashley said, watching him adoringly as he lifted the wheelchair into the back of the car. "You were so sweet to your husband the other night."

It wasn't working — she seemed to be inspiring Ashley in the wrong direction. She'd try Jared, who was tangled up with Ashley again.

"Thank you so much for helping me, Jared," she said. "You'll make a great missionary one day."

"You're welcome," he said.

"I guess you'll be leaving for a mission in a couple of years, won't you?" she said.

"Sure," he answered, squeezing Ashley's shoulders. She was looking down at the ground.

"Well," Allison said. "I guess I'd better get the old car started." She held her car keys up and jiggled them.

"Well, good-bye, Sister Lewis," Ashley said, smiling again. "Tell Brother Lewis hi."

As Allison turned around to get into her car the rest of her family came running out, followed by Liz whose face lit up when she saw Allison beside Ashley. She came quickly over to Allison and grabbed her poor bruised arm again.

"Are you having a nice conversation with my daughter, Sister Lewis?" she said.

"A real nice one," Allison answered. She opened her car door and eased herself behind it, gently taking her arm with her.

"You should listen to Sister Lewis now that she's the Young Women President," Liz said to Ashley.

"I will, Mother," she said obediently. Then, "Can Jared take me home and eat his cake?"

At that Allison jumped into her car and slammed her door. She rolled down her window enough to yell, "Gotta go. 'Bye everyone." Liz bent down to smile and wave at Allison as Allison put her foot to the floor and backed out of the parking place much too quickly.

Before she got very far, though, shouts of "Mother! Mother!" made Allison look back, and she realized she had left Sharon behind. She quickly stopped and, while she waited for Sharon to catch up, slid down in her seat and looked back in her sideview mirror. Liz, Ashley, and Jared were still close together talking but as Allison watched Jared got into his car alone as Liz grabbed Ashley's arm and led her away to their car. Evidently Jared could not share the cake with Ashley.

"Oh no," Allison said. "Liz was not satisfied with my conversation with Ashley."

"Mother," Sharon said, opening the car door. "Are you all right?"

"I'm fine, dear," Allison said. "I'm just anxious to get home and check on Daddy." And take the phone off the hook, she added to herself. Then she took off much too quickly again before Sharon even shut her door.

17

*W*hen Allison and the children reached home Andrew and Mark ran into the house to tell their Daddy all about their exciting evening.

"Sharon, will you make sure the cake gets in the house safely while I get Melinda out?" Allison asked. She hoped as she opened the car door that the boys would forget all about the funniest cake there tonight and think of something else noteworthy to tell Brian about, but she doubted it. But then wasn't that what marriage was all about — sharing all your little humiliations and heartbreaks with each other. It sounded good anyway.

Before she could get the wheelchair out of the car the boys came running back out of the house shouting. "Daddy's on the floor," Andrew said.

"He said help, help," Mark said.

"What's wrong?" Allison almost dropped the wheelchair.

"I don't know," Andrew said. "He's in Matthew's room."

"What's he doing in there?" Allison said. Brian wasn't allowed out of his room. "Sharon, can you get Melinda out while I go check on Daddy?" She raced into the house trying to imagine what could have happened to Brian. She found him, just as Andrew had said, in Matthew's room on the floor between the two beds flat on his back. Matthew was in his bed fast asleep.

"What's wrong?" she said, looking down at him.

"I think I'm dying," he said.

"What's wrong?" she repeated. "Why are you down there?"

"I'm dying because my back is in agony and I can't move."

She reached down and grabbed his arm. "Don't touch me," he yelled.

Allison started to get afraid. She had never seen him like this. She couldn't leave him on the floor squashed between two beds with a Castle Grayskull on his head.

"Honey," she said as calmly as she could. "Where do you hurt?"

"My back and my legs, Allison," he said. Then he tried to move and groaned in pain.

"Don't move," Allison said. "Tell me what happened."

He spoke through clenched teeth. "Matthew fell asleep and wet our bed so I had to bring him in here."

"But you're not supposed to lift anything," she said. She couldn't believe he had done something so stupid.

"I know," he said impatiently. "But I couldn't just let him stay in a wet bed so I picked him up carefully and did just fine until I went to put him on his bed and he twisted around. I tried to catch him but I had a terrible pain in my back. I laid down to wait until it went away but it keeps getting worse. Now my legs are numb."

That scared her to death. She sat down on the bed and tried to calmly think what she should do. "What should I do?" she asked Brian.

"I think I need to go to the hospital," he answered. "But I can't sit up. I think you're going to have to call the rescue squad."

"An ambulance?" she said. She had never had to call an ambulance for a member of her family before.

"I can't stand this pain, Allison," he said. He had broken out in a sweat and looked terribly pale even to Allison's untrained eye.

"Okay," she said, taking a deep breath. She looked over at the door where all the children were standing. Melinda looked like she could burst into tears any moment.

"Andrew, go get a cold washcloth for Daddy and put it on his forehead," she said. "Mark, you stand by Daddy like a real big boy and call me if he wants you to. Sharon, can you take Melinda into her room and put her in her pajamas and turn on a tape or something?" The sound of the siren would probably scare her to death.

The swiftness with which they moved to obey let Allison know how afraid they all were.

"I'll go call the rescue squad, Brian," she said. "Hold on."

The ambulance was there in under ten minutes. She and the children, except Melinda, stood in the hall and watched as the medical technicians briefly examined him and then carefully laid him on a backboard and lifted him onto the stretcher. He was in so much pain that Allison could hardly stand to watch.

"Are you coming with us, ma'am?" one of the technicians asked as they carried him through the hall.

She looked uncertainly down at her children, wondering if they would be all right because she had to go with Brian.

Sharon spoke up quickly. "Go, Mom. We'll be fine. I can take care of everything."

"Sure, Mom," Andrew said. "Sharon can take care of Melinda and I'll watch Mark."

Sharon put her arm around Andrew. "We'll be fine," she said. "Go take care of Daddy."

"Okay," Allison said. "Let me go tell Melinda. Andrew, go tell the men I'll follow in the car."

Andrew sped off as Allison walked into Melinda's room where she was lying on her bed listening to her Cinderella tape. Allison forced herself to sound cheerful because Sharon did not need to have Melinda screaming half the night. "Mommy's going to go with Daddy to the doctor and see what's wrong with Daddy's back, okay?" Melinda nodded, her eyes huge. "Sharon is going to get you ready for bed and maybe if you're real quiet she'll give you some of our cake we bought. Okay?" Melinda nodded again.

Allison kissed her lightly, then walked out without really saying good-bye.

"Sharon, you can cut each of the kids a piece of cake before they go to bed," she said between kisses to each one.

"Okay, Mom," Andrew said. "Just go."

"Mom," Sharon called as Allison opened the door. "Please call us in a little bit and let us know how Daddy is."

"I promise," she said. She ran down to the car to follow the ambulance that was already speeding down the street.

*

By the time Allison found a parking place in the hospital parking lot and reached the emergency room Brian was already inside a cubicle being examined by doctor. She stood for a few minutes in the corner by the curtain until he had finished and motioned her over. "Mrs. Lewis," he said. "I'm Dr. Kandt. I've called in a neurosurgeon to look at your husband."

"A neurosurgeon?" she said. That sounded awful.

"Yes. I think your husband has a slipped disc. He told us that he has been in bed this week because of back pain."

"That's right," she said. "But he was feeling better."

"Sometimes it just takes twisting your back suddenly or even bending over to cause a disc to rupture, especially with a history of back trouble," he said. "We're going to go ahead and admit him tonight and Dr. Bernard will be by later. Do you have any questions?"

"Is he still in a lot of pain?" she asked.

"We've given him something for the pain," he said. "He might be getting a little drowsy but you can stay with him now."

"Thank you," she said as he walked away. She walked over to Brian who was lying with his eyes closed. When she picked up his hand to hold, he opened his eyes and smiled up at her.

"Are you feeling better?" she asked.

"Just a little. Who's watching the kids?"

"Sharon."

"How much is it costing us?"

"Nothing, honey," she said. "They're worried about you."

"I'm worried about me," he said. "I've never hurt so much. How do you stand to have babies?"

"I've wondered that myself."

"What time is it?" he asked, trying to look at her watch.

"A little after nine."

"I'm missing Dallas," he said.

"Brian!" She was scared to death and he was still crazy. She looked at him for a few minutes, shaking her head in exasperation. Then she remembered she was supposed to call the children so she stood up and searched for a quarter in her purse. "I'll go call Sharon and you try to rest," she said. "And don't worry about Dallas. You can catch it on the reruns."

As she searched for a pay phone she turned a corner and ran right into Bishop Murphy and Brother Parker.

"Allison," Bishop Murphy said. "Sharon called me at church and told me about Brian. How is he? We thought he might need a blessing."

"Oh thank you," she said. She told them what the doctor had said. "They'll tell you at the desk where he is. I've just got to go call the children."

"We'll find it," the bishop said. "Don't worry." He started down the hall the way they had come in until

Brother Parker grabbed his arm and said, "This way, Bishop. That's the way we came in."

They had already left by the time she had finished telling Sharon every little detail. Brian was lying quietly.

"Brian," she whispered. "Did the bishop find you?"

He nodded his head slowly.

Before he lost complete consciousness she had to know about the blessing. "Did they administer to you?" she asked.

He nodded again.

"Was it a blessing that you would be healed or did they just say that you would have strength to endure this?"

She listened for his answer, which was quiet when it came. "I don't know," he said. "I don't remember. My back was hurting too much."

"Okay," she said. She picked up his hand and laid her cheek against it. She would be quiet and let him rest until they came to get him.

A few minutes later two male attendants came to wheel him up to his room. Allison followed silently, her head hurting from the bright lights and her heart hurting from the pain her husband was in.

Within a half an hour a nurse bustled in, followed by a tall, thin doctor who introduced himself as Dr. Bernard. Allison stood up to watch from the end of the bed as Dr. Bernard examined Brian. He didn't say anything until he had finished and carefully put away his rubber hammer he had hit Brian everywhere with. Clasping Brian on the shoulder, he turned to Allison.

"Well," he began. "I agree with the diagnosis Dr. Kandt gave you in the emergency room. I believe Brian has at least one ruptured disc; however, we will do a CAT Scan and a myelogram in the morning to confirm it." He explained further. "A CAT Scan is a three dimensional x-ray of the spinal column and a myelogram is a procedure where we inject dye into the veins and take x-rays."

Allison must have looked about as scared as she felt because Dr. Bernard said, "Don't worry, neither of these procedures is very painful."

"Then what?" Brian asked.

"We'll talk about it then," the doctor said. "I'll order traction and pain medication to help you rest tonight." Then he was gone.

Allison walked around to Brian. "Are you okay, honey?"

"I'll be fine," he said. "Now why don't you go home and see about the children."

"I hate to leave you," she said.

"We'll take good care of him," the nurse said. "We're going to string his legs up with some weights and knock him out with a shot. You go home, get some rest, and come back tomorrow."

"Go on," he said. He put his hand over hers.

"Well, okay," she said reluctantly. "I'll leave our number at the desk and you have them call me if you need me." She bent down to kiss him, blinking away tears. She had never been very good at good-byes, especially when the person she was saying it to looked so pale and helpless in his hospital bed.

"He'll be just fine," the nurse said.

"Okay, I'm going," she said. She started for the door.

"Tell the kids I love them," Brian said.

"I will." She shut the door quietly and walked down the hall. This was the first time Brian had been in the hospital since they'd been married and she didn't like it one bit. She had never felt so alone.

When she walked in the door at home all was quiet. Thank goodness, she thought, no screaming Melinda.

"I'm in here, Mom," Sharon called from the family room.

"Be right there," Allison said. Tiptoeing down the hall, she checked first on Melinda then on the two little ones. They were all asleep, but Andrew's bed was empty.

She walked back to the family room to find Sharon curled up in an afghan reading a magazine and Andrew curled up in front of the TV fast asleep.

"How's Daddy?" Sharon asked.

"He's not in quite as much pain," Allison said. "They gave him a shot and were getting ready to put him in traction when I left. They are going to do some tests first thing in the morning to make sure he has a ruptured disc."

"Then what?" Sharon asked. She looked so upset that Allison sat down beside her on the couch.

"The doctor wouldn't say," Allison said. "He said we'd talk about it after the tests."

"Do you think he'll have to have surgery?" Sharon asked.

"I don't know, honey. I just don't know." Then just as tears welled up in her eyes and threatened to spill over Sharon started sobbing, so Allison put her arms around her and pulled Sharon over to her. "He'll be okay, Sharon. The bishop administered to him tonight and we'll just have to have faith that he'll be okay."

"But what if he's paralyzed?" Sharon sobbed.

"Oh honey," Allison said, holding her even closer. "I don't think that's a possibility." She didn't remember reading about that in those back trouble books. Maybe she'd have to go read them again.

Sharon calmed down a little. Allison rubbed her back and said, "Now dry those tears and help me figure out who can help take care of all these kids I have."

Sharon sat up, wiping her eyes. "I didn't tell you," she said. "Sister Parker called and told me to tell you that she would have at least two Relief Society sisters over early in the morning to take care of the kids and not to worry about meals — they will bring them in."

"But what about Melinda?" Allison asked. "I guess I could call her aide from school to come and take care of her."

"You don't have to do that, Mom. I'll be here — I'll help take care of her."

Allison looked over at her suspiciously and smiled. "But how much will it cost me?"

Sharon smiled back. "It won't cost anything. We did fine tonight. Andrew even fed Melinda some cake — he didn't give her any M&Ms so she wouldn't choke." She hesitated, then added, "I changed the sheets afterwards. They're in the dryer."

"I've got some good kids," Allison said, hugging Sharon. "If you'll just make sure that Melinda is happy and that the Disastrous Duo doesn't do much damage, I'll do something great for you when this is over with." She stood up and sighed tiredly. "Maybe Daddy will feel better tomorrow." She folded up the afghan neatly like she did every night, so it would be ready to be unfolded first thing in the morning. "Now let's get some sleep, young lady. I think we both have a rough day coming tomorrow."

She roused Andrew up from the floor and half-carried, half-pushed him down the hall to his bedroom. She was so tired that she couldn't wait to get into bed. But even as she longed for sleep she knew it wouldn't come easily tonight.

18

*A*llison didn't know what time the sisters were coming so she got all the children up early to have them fed and dressed by eight-thirty. At the breakfast table she told them about their Daddy and gave them a pep talk about their behavior for the day ahead.

"Matthew and Mark — I guess you can watch a lot of cartoons today," she said. "And if you get tired of TV then go outside and play." They loved the cartoon idea so much they jumped up and down, which made Allison feel guilty. "Enjoy it today," she added. "Because it won't happen often."

She turned to Andrew whom she didn't really have to worry about — he was good at entertaining himself. "Will you help keep Melinda happy?" Saturdays at home tended to be long days for Melinda with her limited abilities to play. "Maybe get her Play-Doh out."

"Okay, Mom," he said. "I'll be her recreation director today."

She rumpled his still-rumpled hair and turned to Sharon. "Sharon, you sort of play Mommy but don't be too bossy."

"Mother. I'm not bossy."

"You know what I mean," Allison said. "Let the sisters be in charge but help them. And don't let anyone go in my linen closet."

"I think they're here," Andrew said, looking out the window.

"Who is it?" Allison asked.

"Sister McFarren and Sister Parker," Andrew said.

"Sister McFarren," Sharon groaned. "She always pinches my cheek and tells me how sweet I am."

"Well, be sweet then," Allison said. "I'll be home as soon as I can." She picked up the suitcase she had packed early that morning and contemplated her children. She didn't want to leave them but she had to be with Brian. If only Melinda could play or color or do any of the other things six year old girls did to occupy themselves while their mothers were gone she wouldn't worry so much.

Oh well, she thought, squaring her shoulders. If it weren't an emergency I wouldn't be leaving them. I'll make it up to them later.

After blowing everyone a kiss, she let the sisters in as she left.

Brian wasn't in his room when she got there. The empty bed with the neatly-made sheets gave her a scare until a nurse came quickly into the room and explained that he had gone early for his tests and would be back soon.

By the time Allison unpacked his suitcase and was halfway through reading the pamphlet on hospital policy and procedure the door opened and two attendants wheeled Brian through. He moaned loudly as they hit the side of the door. She knew Brian wouldn't want her to hear him crying out in pain, so she ducked into the bathroom and stayed there until they had transferred him to his bed. He moaned several times in the process.

When the attendants had left she stepped out and quickly went over to where he was lying with his arm over his face.

"Hi," she said. Putting her hand on his arm, she bent down to kiss him.

"Oh hi," he said, too surprised to return the kiss. "How long have you been here?"

"Just a few minutes," she said. "How were the tests?"

"Terrible."

"But I thought the doctor said that they wouldn't be painful." She sat down and picked up his hand to hold.

"The tests weren't painful," he explained. "But lying on that hard cold table and having to be still was horrible. I almost passed out."

Brian had always been so strong and healthy that she found it hard to picture him fainting. She had come this morning hoping to find him feeling better but he seemed to feel worse.

"What did the doctor say?" she asked.

"He just said he'd read the results and be by in a little bit."

"Do you want something to eat?" she asked. "Your breakfast is over there."

"No. I can't eat right now. But call the nurse and see if I can have more pain medication."

"Is it time for more?"

"I don't care," he said. "I just want to stop hurting."

Not long after the nurse brought in what she called Brian's "happy pills" Dr. Bernard came in looking very serious. Allison knew as soon as she saw the expression on his face that she was not going to like what he said. He pulled up a chair beside her and cleared his throat.

"Brian," he began. "You have a messed-up back. The tests show at least two ruptured discs and what looks like scar tissue from either a previous injury or a congenital problem. It's no wonder you're in such pain." He was quiet a few minutes, looking down at his chart.

Allison felt her stomach tighten up like it always did when she was nervous. She took a deep breath, though, and asked, "So, what can you do about it?"

He looked up from his chart. "The best treatment is surgery," he said. "We can go in, remove the discs, and relieve the pressure on the nerves causing the pain. We might need to remove some scar tissue, too." He looked over at Brian who hadn't said anything yet. "What do you think of that, Brian?"

"If this pain will go away I want you to do it," he said. "I can't stand this much longer."

"When would you do the surgery, doctor?" Allison asked. "Tomorrow?"

"This afternoon," he said.

Her stomach really started shaking. "I thought doctors played golf on Saturday afternoons," she said. She knew as soon as she heard what she said how stupid it sounded.

But the doctor laughed. "That's Wednesdays," he said. "Besides, I just couldn't go play golf this afternoon knowing what pain Brian is in, could I?" Then he got serious again. "This isn't a life-threatening situation but there is no reason to wait so we'll go ahead and set the surgery up and see if we can't get Brian feeling better. Okay?"

He stood up and moved closer to Brian. "Any questions?"

"When can you knock me out?"

A few minutes after that, when the nurses took over the room to begin to prep Brian for his surgery, Allison decided to call home and tell them about the surgery. She slipped out of the room and walked down the hall to the pay phone.

"Hi, honey," Allison said when Sharon answered the phone. "How's everything?"

"Just great, Mom."

"What's Melinda doing?"

"She's fine, too," Sharon said. "Sister McFarren has her outside in her wheelchair watching the boys play."

"Is her seat belt on?"

"Of course, Mom. I put it on. Now how's Daddy?"

That was going to be difficult to answer. Allison somehow had to mask her own fears to not alarm the children. It would be easier if she could be there with them. "Now don't worry," she began. "The neurosurgeon said that he has a ruptured disc and he needs an operation to remove the disc."

"Surgery?" Sharon asked.

"Yes, honey," she answered. "In fact, they're getting him ready to go to surgery now. But the doctor says it's a common operation and Daddy should do just fine."

"Okay," Sharon said bravely. "I'll tell the other kids for you. Just call us when you know something."

"You know I will, honey. Do you have anything for supper?"

"Sister Parker called to say not to worry about food — the Relief Society will take care of that." Then she added, in a whisper, "Andrew and I are glad that Sister Murphy is here babysitting and not home cooking."

Allison laughed softly. "I'd better get back to Daddy. Call me here if you need me. And take good care of everyone."

"Melinda will be fine, Mom," Sharon assured her. "Bye-bye."

"One more thing, Sharon."

"What?"

"Why don't you children have a special prayer for Daddy?"

"We already did, but we'll have another one."

Allison hung up the phone and walked slowly down the hall. She could still see the nurses in Brian's room so she sat down in the waiting room and tried to pull herself together. She knew she should be strong for Brian and the children now, but she hadn't felt so weak and upset since they had first found out about Melinda. But then Brian had been with her and had given her strength when hers had run out. Somehow since that terrible time she had found the courage she needed to face the daily heartache that came with having a handicapped child, but now she felt like she had no strength or courage left to cope with something being wrong with Brian.

She sat quietly, without tears, hugging her pocketbook on her lap. She hated crying in front of people so she decided right then that she wouldn't cry until all this was over with and Brian was up on his feet again. Then he could put his arms around her and she would cry until there were no tears left. She thought about what Sister McFarren had said last Sunday. If people thought she was strong maybe she could be. In fact, she had to be — the children and Brian needed her and she was going to be there for them. There was really no one else.

Standing up, she started toward Brian's room, praying silently that she could indeed be what she had decided to be. She clutched her pocketbook to her chest and put what she hoped was a brave smile on her face.

For a moment when she first saw him her resolve weakened just a bit but she walked over to him and, leaving her pocketbook on a chair, picked up his left hand. His right hand now had an intravenous tube in it connected to a bottle of clear liquid hanging over his bed. He had on a clean white hospital gown with a green surgical cap covering his hair.

"You look cute," she said.

"Hi, honey," he said. "How are the kids?" His words were a little slurred.

Allison looked up at the nurse with a question in her eyes.

"He's had two shots to relax him for the surgery," she explained to Allison.

"Well, you're certainly relaxed," Allison joked with him. She let his hand go and it flopped to the bed. He smiled weakly and closed his eyes again, so she gently put his hand under the sheet and sat down.

It was only a few minutes later that the surgical attendants came and wheeled him out of his room. Allison walked beside his stretcher holding his hand. They all crowded into an elevator and rode down two floors. When they came out they were on the surgical wing and Dr. Bernard was waiting for them.

"There's a comfortable waiting room right down the hall here," he said to Allison. "You can wait there and I'll come speak with you when we have him all fixed up."

Allison could only nod because the tears she had decided not to shed were choking her throat.

"Tell your pretty wife good-bye, Brian," Dr. Bernard said. "When you see her again you'll be a new man."

Brian squeezed Allison's hand and mumbled, "Don't worry, honey, I'll be okay."

Allison nodded again before she leaned down and quickly kissed him on the forehead.

Then with a feeble attempt to wave to her he disappeared behind the wide doors and she was alone. She stood there for a few seconds until the lump in her throat was gone, then looked around for the waiting room. The door was right behind her.

She had her choice of seats when she walked in because the room was deserted. Picking up an old *Field and Stream* magazine, she chose a seat across from the door so she could see the doctor as soon as he came in.

An old movie was droning on the black and white TV sitting on a coffee table. After a few minutes of dividing her fitful attention between the old magazine and the old movie, Allison decided that when she got rich she was going to donate a color TV and subscriptions to ten interesting magazines to the surgical waiting room.

An hour, then two hours passed as Allison waited. She called home twice to say she hadn't heard anything yet and was glad to hear that Melinda and the boys had decided to take long naps. Then she paced a little, tried to get interested in a tennis tournament, and drank the only decaffeinated drink that was in the drink machine. It was times like this she regretted living so far away from any family. At least she'd have someone to wait with her.

The nurse had said the surgery would take about three hours so she was surprised to hear the door open after only two and a half as she stood looking out the window. She whirled around to see Bishop Murphy peeking around the door.

"Is this the surgical waiting room?" he asked. "Well, I guess it really doesn't matter, does it? Because if this is where you are then this is where I should be even if it isn't the surgical waiting room. Right?"

"Right, bishop," she said, smiling for the first time since she'd been there. "Come on in."

He came on in, shutting the door gently behind him. She walked across the room to meet him and put her hand into his outstretched one. She felt strange shaking his hand here and he must have read her thoughts because he pulled her close and enveloped her in a big hug.

"I'm so sorry, so sorry, Allison," he said. "But I just know he's going to be fine. I have a good feeling about it." He let her go and looked down at her as she stood not saying a word. "I have faith in the blessing Charlie and I gave him. I have a good feeling about it and you should too."

"I do," she said. "But neither of us have ever had surgery before and I guess I'm just nervous."

"And you should be," he said. "I don't mean real nervous — just nervous enough to care, which I'm sure you would anyway even if you weren't nervous. Which you are. Nervous, I mean. Right?" He nodded his head as if agreeing with himself.

She decided to let him figure the answer to that out himself. "Would you like something to drink?" she asked.

She had only been there a couple of hours and already she was acting like the mother of the waiting room.

"No thanks," he said. "Don't go to any trouble. I just wanted to come and be with you since you were here by yourself."

"I really appreciate it, bishop," she said. "I was feeling real alone."

"Well, let's just sit and be together then," he said. "After all, we're the only ones in here who can be together. So we may as well." They settled down into the two seats across from the door.

The good thing about the bishop being there was that she had the comfort of a caring person beside her but she didn't really have to listen too carefully to the long rambling stories he was entertaining her with. An occasional nod and smile in his direction kept him going while she worried and wondered what was keeping the doctor so long.

It had been about three and a half hours when the door finally opened and Dr. Bernard walked in. Allison jumped up with the bishop behind her, trying to read the doctor's face as she walked over to meet him.

"He did real well, Mrs. Lewis," he said quickly. "We removed two discs and some scar tissue."

Allison breathed a sigh of relief. "Then he's okay?"

"He's in the recovery room now and should be back in his room in a couple of hours," he said. "It was no wonder he's been in such pain. There was a lot of inflammation in his spinal sac and we had to go in there to relieve it. We're going to be watching him real closely."

She didn't like the sound of that. "But I thought you said he was okay?"

"He is," Dr. Bernard assured her. "But we want him to continue to do well so we'll be watching him closely. He had a lot of work done."

"Thank you so much," she said.

He nodded, then said, "Why don't you go wait in his room now where you can be more comfortable?"

Allison and Bishop Murphy followed his advice and went back up to Brian's room where Allison called home to tell the children that their Daddy was fine. Another set of sisters had taken over the babysitting duties and were getting supper ready. Sharon continued to assure Allison that Melinda was happy so Allison accepted her word because she just didn't want to have anyone else to worry about.

They had waited about an hour when Bishop Murphy said, "I think I'll go home. Brian doesn't need to see me here when he comes back. Unless you want me to stay and then I will or you can call me if you need me."

"I will," she said.

"Need me?" he asked.

"No, I'll call you if I need you," she said. "But I know I won't. Need you, I mean." She couldn't believe it — a couple of hours with him and she was beginning to talk like him. "I really appreciate you coming and staying with me, Bishop. It helped having someone there."

"I was glad," he said. "Not glad about Brian but glad I could be here if things had to be like they are." He took her hand in a handshake with both of his hands. "You call me if you need me."

She was not going to get involved with that again so she nodded her head and smiled.

"I'll go home and help Sister Murphy get some food together for your family."

"Oh, please, please, don't worry about that," she begged.

"I won't," he said. "Worry, that is. I'll just go do it."

That was what worried her. She walked him into the hall, thanking him again, then walked back into the room and made sure that Brian's sheets were straight and wrinkle-free. Maybe she should have been a nurse.

She couldn't wait to see him but at the same time she dreaded it because she didn't know what kind of shape he'd be in. She had never had surgery but she knew how she felt after having a baby and it wasn't good.

And he didn't look too good when he was brought in a little while later. The nurses asked her to leave while they transferred him from the stretcher to his bed but from the hallway she could hear him moan as they moved him. When she went back in a nurse explained that he would have an IV in probably until the morning and that the tube coming from his back was a drainage tube from his incision. She knew as she looked at it and her stomach rolled that she should not have been a nurse.

Brian was pale and groggy although he did manage a weak, "Hi, babe," when she walked up beside him.

"The question is how are you?" she said.

"How do I look?"

"About as bad as you feel."

Sitting down beside him she pulled her chair up as close to the bed as possible and stared at him as he immediately went to sleep.

That was where she stayed until late into the evening. She picked at Brian's dinner because he was not at all interested in it. He slept for an hour or two at a time, waking up only to ask for a drink of water or to ask if she was still there.

Dr. Bernard came in around nine o'clock, looking over his chart and checking the tubes. When he finished he looked over at Allison kindly. "You've had a long day, Mrs. Lewis. Why don't you go home and get some rest?"

"I hate to leave him," she said.

"He's in good hands and according to his chart he's doing fine for a person who had the kind of surgery he had." He glanced back down at the chart, then looked up again quizzically. "Didn't someone tell me you have a bunch of kids?"

"We have five."

"Then why don't you go home and tell them good-night. You can get some sleep and be back early in the morning. He should be more awake by that time."

The mention of the children convinced her to take his advice. Becky had assured her the last time she called home that she wouldn't mind spending the night at all, but Allison really would like the children to know that she hadn't forgotten them.

The nurses promised her — several times — that they would take good care of him and call if anything at all didn't look good. Before she left she shook Brian awake gently to a semi-conscious state and told him she was going home to check on the children. He drowsily assured her that he would be fine. So, she reluctantly left, wishing as she climbed into her car that she could be in two places at the same time.

When she pulled up into the driveway at home all the lights were on which was not a good sign. She heard shouts of "Mommy's home, Mommy's home!" as she walked up on the porch. The door was barely open before two little Supermen grabbed her around the knees. As she struggled to maintain her balance Andrew grabbed her around her neck. They all fell in a laughing heap on the floor. Trying to hug all three boys at once, she looked up from the floor to see Sharon pushing Melinda up to her.

Allison disentangled all the little arms from around her neck and gathered Matthew and Mark onto her lap as she sat up somewhat straight.

"Hi, Melinda," Allison said. "Were you good while Mommy was gone?"

"She was real good," Becky said, coming up behind Sharon.

"I told you so," Sharon said. "She worries a lot," she said to Becky.

"That's what mothers get paid for," Becky answered.

Allison unbuckled Melinda and picked her up, holding her close. All the children talked at once telling her what they had done that day and she told them how brave their Daddy had been and that it would be no time at all until he was home without his back hurting.

Then they dragged her into the kitchen and showed her all the food the Relief Society had brought over which they had neatly lined up on the kitchen table and stacked in the refrigerator.

"And this is the yucky stuff," Mark said. He pointed to four or five dishes on the counter closest to the trash can. "We're not going to eat that."

"Mark!" Allison said, looking over at Becky with embarrassment.

"Don't worry," Becky said. "My food made the refrigerator." She picked Mark up and tickled him in the stomach. "But remember, we aren't going to tell anyone that we didn't like some of the food they so nicely brought over, are we?"

"Cross my heart," he said, crossing his heart.

Melinda was beginning to get a little heavy in Allison's arms. She shifted her to her other shoulder and said, "Let's go to our bedrooms and I'll read everyone a story before you go to sleep."

"I bet you're exhausted," Becky said. She grabbed a couple of kids and started out of the kitchen.

"I sure am," Allison said. "I'm going to take a hot shower, call the hospital, and get some sleep." The hot shower and phone call she was sure about. She only wished she could be as sure about the sleep.

19

$\mathcal{T}$he hot shower felt wonderful and the phone call was reassuring — the two combined to put Allison to sleep as soon as she lay down. She slept soundly and dreamlessly until four in the morning when she was suddenly wide awake, knowing that someone was about to need her. It was the same feeling she always had when she had a new baby in the house and woke knowing that the baby was about to cry for her. She lay in bed, listening for a couple of minutes but when she didn't hear anyone she got up and walked down the hall, peeking into everyone's room. But all the children were sleeping peacefully.

The feeling persisted, though, as she walked into the kitchen to get a drink of water. As she drank her water she looked over at the phone and decided that since she was up she may as well call the hospital to check on Brian. But as she put her glass down the phone rang loudly in the silence of the house and she knew with a tightening in her throat that this was the reason she was awake and waiting. Something was wrong with Brian.

She grabbed the phone up with a desperate hello.

"Mrs. Lewis," a calm voice said.

"Yes?"

"This is Nurse Kincaid from the hospital. Please don't get upset but we are having a little trouble with your husband's blood pressure and we thought you might want to know."

"What's wrong with it?" Allison asked.

"He's not in any real danger but his blood pressure has been awfully low the last couple of hours and we are getting ready to give him some blood. We've called Dr. Bernard and he said he'll be in in a little while to check him over to make sure everything is fine."

"I'll be right there," Allison said.

"Don't rush," the nurse said. "There's no immediate danger. The nurses last shift told us we were to call you if anything changed."

"Thank you," Allison said. "I'll be right there."

She hung up the phone, her mind racing. Becky had begged her to call her during the night if she needed her, but it was so early in the morning. She hesitated a minute, then dialed Becky's number. She really had no choice.

"I'll be right there," Becky said after Allison explained the situation to her.

"I'm sorry," Allison apologized for the third time.

"Don't worry about it," Becky answered. "Wake Sharon up to wait for me and I'll be right there."

Allison was at the hospital within twenty minutes. The nurse might have said there was nothing to get upset about but as soon as she walked into Brian's room she was upset. The bright lights were on over his bed as two nurses bent over him. One was checking his blood pressure and the other was busy with the tube now connecting Brian to a bag of blood. She couldn't even see his head at first because his bed was tilted to elevate his feet.

The nurses were so busy that they didn't notice Allison as she hesitated at the door trying to still her racing heart. This seemed like a nightmare to her — the bright hospital lights, the blood, and the nurses efficient as they worked over their patient. And the worst of the nightmare was that their patient was her Brian.

"Oh Mrs. Lewis, you're here," one of the nurses said. She took off the stethoscope she had been monitoring Brian's blood pressure with. "You can come see your husband."

Allison walked over slowly. "How's his blood pressure?"

"It's too low for us not to be concerned. But hopefully, the transfusion will bring it up." She headed for the door but turned back. "We're checking it every five minutes so we'll be back in again soon."

They both left and Allison went over to Brian. His eyes were closed but he opened them and managed a smile when she kissed him. "Sorry to get you up so early," he said.

"I was up waiting for your call," she said lightly. He looked terrible. He was no longer pale — he was absolutely gray. The sweat was dripping off of him so she wet a washcloth with cold water and wiped his forehead.

"That feels good," he said.

"Are you trying to ruin my day or is it just working out that way?" she joked.

"I don't know. I feel lousy."

For the next hour she sat, wiping his forehead and giving him sips of ice water. Every five minutes the nurses came in to check his blood pressure which seemed determined to stay low.

About their tenth time in, Dr. Bernard was with them. He walked to the foot of the bed, picked up Brian's chart, and read it for several minutes before he finally said anything.

When he finally looked up he smiled at Allison. She thought it looked forced. Then he walked around to Brian. "So you're not feeling too good, Brian?"

"Pretty lousy," Brian said.

"We've got to get this blood pressure up," Dr. Bernard said. "Let me check you over a little bit and see if we can find out what the problem is."

One of the nurses came around to Allison's side of the bed so Allison stood up and moved her chair back. "I'll wait in the hall," she said.

She walked down the hall to the nearest window and leaned against it. Looking out at the peacefulness of the early morning she was jealous of all the people still sleeping for whom this was going to be just another normal day. She put her head against the cool of the glass because her head was killing her.

Dr. Bernard clearing his throat beside her interrupted her thoughts. "Mrs. Lewis, I think we know what the problem is."

"What?"

"Brian seems to be leaking some spinal cord fluid from his incision. Actually, it's a large amount."

"Why? What is causing that?"

"Well, as I told you, I had to go into his spinal sac and that is very difficult to stitch back up. Very rarely the stitches pull loose for some reason and let the spinal fluid escape. Evidently that's what happened in Brian's case."

"What can you do about it?" It sounded terrible, but if Dr. Bernard was familiar with this type of problem then surely he knew what to do about it.

"I would like it to clear up by itself, but if it doesn't soon, we'll have to go back in and restitch it. The longer this goes on the more chance there is of spinal meningitis setting in."

"Spinal meningitis?" she asked, not wanting to believe what she was hearing. People died from that. Allison felt weak all of a sudden and sat down in the nearest chair.

"Are you all right, Mrs. Lewis?" Dr. Bernard leaned over her. She nodded her head. "Please try not to worry. We're going to keep a very close eye on him and not take any chances. Are you sure you're all right?"

"Yes," she said. "I've just got a terrible headache."

"Well, you go to the nurses' station and tell them I said to give you some aspirin, then you try to relax. We're taking good care of him. Don't worry."

He walked away.

Don't worry, she thought. He uses words like spinal meningitis and tells me not to worry? It was her husband in there, the father of those children of hers at home and she could worry if she wanted to. She was worried sick.

By afternoon Allison felt like the day had already been a week long. Brian had developed a tremendous headache from the spinal cord leakage so Dr. Bernard had prescribed a strong painkiller for him which kept him groggy.

Since her children had been born, especially Melinda, she had longed for occasional days when she had nothing more to do than read magazines and watch TV. Now she had a day like that and she would gladly trade it for her usual busy Sunday of church and children. She'd even go through the sacrament meeting program again if only Brian were all right.

As she replaced the phone gently about three o'clock Brian opened his eyes. "How are the kids?" he asked.

"Fine," she said. "Becky moved her whole family into our house for the afternoon after church. She said everything is going well. Melinda and the boys are still asleep."

"I can't believe you are leaving Melinda for so long," he mumbled.

"Me neither. But I can't leave you since you've decided to complicate your surgery."

He smiled weakly. "I love you."

"I love you, too," she said. Then her resolve weakened so much at his words that it disappeared and tears came spilling out. She glanced at Brian but he had closed his eyes again and hadn't seen her tears. Wiping them away and taking deep breaths to stop any more from coming, she walked over to the small window to look out.

She was trying to be brave but she was so afraid that she was going to lose Brian. Since Melinda had been born she hadn't worried much about something happening to Brian because she assumed that Melinda's handicap was her big trial and tribulation in life and there would be no more major ones. Maybe she had assumed wrong. Maybe she had been such a strong spirit in the preexistence that she had agreed to accept a bunch of trials and tribulations. What had Sister McFarren called her? A rock. Maybe she had been a rock in the preexistence. If she had been, she sure didn't feel like one now.

As she turned away from the window Dr. Bernard walked in and went immediately over to check the dressing on Brian's back. She tried to hear what he and the nurse were saying but they were speaking too quietly. From the way he was shaking his head, though, Allison knew it couldn't be good news. She walked over and stood at the foot of the bed holding onto the bottom railing tightly for support.

Dr. Bernard came around and sat in the chair beside Brian. He put his hand on Brian's shoulder. "How are you feeling, Brian?"

Brian opened his eyes and squinted up at Dr. Bernard. "Terrible. My head and back are killing me."

Dr. Bernard was quiet as he looked up at Allison and back down at Brian. Then he said slowly, "I think we have to go back in and take care of this leak. It isn't clearing up on its own — in fact, it's gotten worse. That's why you're feeling worse, Brian."

"Then do it now," Brian said. "This pain is beginning to bother me."

Dr. Bernard looked up at Allison questioningly. She nodded her head silently, the lump in her throat standing in the way of any words.

"I'll see you soon then," he said to Brian. He patted his shoulder again and stood up. "We'll take care of him," he told Allison again, patting her shoulder as he walked by. Then he left.

20

A few minutes after Allison lay down on the vinyl couch in the surgical waiting room, the door opened and Sharon, Becky, and Andrew came in. Allison sat up, running her fingers through her hair. She knew that she must look awful.

Andrew confirmed it. "You look terrible, Mom."

"Thanks," she said, putting an arm around each of them. "You look pretty good to me."

"She's tired, Andrew," Sharon said.

Becky settled herself into one of the chairs. "Everyone was settled in bed and almost asleep when we left. And we are staying here until you know Brian is okay. You've been alone too much."

"I appreciate it," Allison said. She felt much better with them here.

Becky and Sharon picked up magazines to flip through and Andrew found something interesting to him on the TV. Allison tried both but soon put her head back against the wall consumed with thoughts she didn't particularly want to think about. In her mind she acted out how she would react if Dr. Bernard came in with bad news. When that became too upsetting to think about, she thought back to their temple wedding, feeling gratitude once more for the eternity part of their marriage but praying that they would still have lots of the time part left together. She longed to doze off but she just couldn't do it. Every part of her strained, but dreaded, to hear the sound of footsteps in front of the waiting room door.

They heard voices coming down the hall. Allison recognized one as Dr. Bernard's. She jumped up. Sharon put down her magazine and came over to her, putting her arm around her mother's shoulders. Becky turned off the TV and sat down beside Andrew.

Finally the voices and the footsteps stopped in front of their room, and the door opened. Dr. Bernard's face was expressionless as he crossed the room to Allison.

When he stopped in front of her, however, his face broke into a smile. "Brian should be just fine, Mrs. Lewis. He came through the surgery real well and we had no trouble repairing the tear."

"Oh thank you," Allison said, suddenly weak with relief. "Thank you." Then, as much as she tried to hold them back the tears came as she hugged Sharon and Andrew.

"You look so much better," Allison said to Brian for at least the hundredth time. He had been back in his room only an hour and already his cheeks had some pink in them. His headache had eased enough that he was able to doze off and on.

"I feel so much better," he told her for the hundredth time.

She kissed his hand she hadn't let go of since she had gotten it. "I'm so glad you're okay. You can watch all the soap operas you want to and I won't even fuss. I'll even pick up your dirty clothes the rest of my life without fussing."

"Don't go too far," he said. "You might promise something you'll regret later." He squeezed her hand.

She considered what he said. "You're right. But I know I won't regret saying this."

"What?"

"I love you."

"I love you, too," he said. Then, overcome with the passion of the moment, he fell asleep and started snoring — the one thing Allison would never promise not to complain about.

21

*A*fter a week and a half Allison had shifted comfortably into a routine of mornings at home and afternoons at the hospital while a willing sister sat with her napping children. The sisters were more willing when the children were napping. Then back home to fix supper and hear Andrew's and Sharon's school problems, and a quick trip to the hospital in the evening while Sharon and one of the Young Women babysat.

I'm doing real well, Allison thought to herself as she prepared to go to the hospital the evening before Brian was to come home. The kitchen was cleaned up — so what if Chef Boy-ar-Dee had cooked their supper. The children's pajamas were laid out for Sharon and Ashley to put on them. And she and the little guys had even made cookies this morning to take to Brian.

She heard the doorbell ring as she searched under the bed for her other shoe. "I could needlepoint a new couch in all the time I spend hunting for shoes," she muttered from under the dust ruffle.

Just as she spied the shoe and reached for it Sharon knocked on her bedroom door. "Mother," she said. "You've got to come out here. Ashley's crying."

"Oh no," Allison said, not coming out from under the bed. She had hoped she wouldn't have to do anything official and inspiring as Young Women President until Brian was home.

"Mother! What are you doing under there? I said Ashley is crying."

"Here I come," Allison said, backing herself out, shoe in hand. She stood up and faced Sharon. "Is her mother with her?"

"No."

"Are you sure?"

"Yes."

"Did she say what was wrong?"

"No. I just said hi and asked her how she was and she said fine, then burst into tears." She grabbed Allison's hand and dragged her out of the room and down the hall. "Come on."

"I'm coming," Allison said, hobbling down the hall with one shoe on and one shoe off.

Ashley was sitting on the couch in the living room sobbing into a tissue as Matthew and Mark stood solemnly before her. "She's crying, Mommy," Mark said.

"I know, honey," Allison answered. "Now can you go into the family room with Sharon and let Mommy talk to Ashley?"

"Mother," Sharon said, not wanting to leave.

"Sharon, go into the family room." Allison watched while Sharon and the boys left, then she turned to Ashley. "What's wrong, dear?" she asked gently. "Did you have a fight with Jared?" A fight with Jared she could handle.

"No," Ashley said.

That left Allison with no choice but to ask the question she already knew the answer to. "Did you have a fight with your mother?"

"Yes," Ashley said. "Oh Sister Lewis, I wish you were my mother. You're so nice."

"No I'm not," Allison said quickly. "Sharon doesn't always think so."

"My mother is so mean."

"What did she do to make you so upset? You don't have to tell me if you don't want to."

But she wanted to. "Oh Sister Lewis, my mother says she's going to take all my money away. She says I'm going to waste my money on marrying Jared."

"What money, dear?" If it was her allowance then Ashley would be disappointed to find out how many times Allison had withheld Sharon's allowance.

"My Daddy's been putting money in a savings account for me ever since I was little and I've put most of my babysitting money in there. I've saved up about two thousand dollars." Ashley looked up at Allison so sadly that Allison put her arm around her. "She found my bank book today in my desk and said she's going to take all my money out so I can't use it to marry Jared."

"Is her name on it?"

"Yes," Ashley said. "I'd forgotten all about it. My father's out of town or he wouldn't let her do that."

Allison didn't want to know the answer to the question that was inside her begging to be asked. But she knew she had to, so she did. "Were you going to use the money to get married after you graduated? You don't have to tell me if you don't want to."

"Yes," Ashley said. "But I love Jared, Sister Lewis, and he loves me."

"I know," Allison said. In fact, she knew entirely too much now. All she had wanted to do was go to the hospital and visit Brian. Now she was stuck smack in the middle of a romantic triangle. She kept patting Ashley on the back as she tried to figure out how she could help without alienat-

ing either Ashley or Liz, but she had a feeling she could sit
there all night and not come up with a way.

"Well," she began carefully. "I'm sure your mother
doesn't hate Jared. She just thinks you're too young to get
married. Don't you think seventeen is just a little too young
for marriage?"

"I'll be eighteen when I graduate. You were eighteen
when you got married."

"I was almost nineteen," Allison said. Big deal. She
started patting and thinking again.

"Doesn't Jared want to go on a mission? Couldn't you
wait until after he comes home?"

"But we'd be married in the temple and that's a
commandment, too."

"Well," Allison said. "That's true, but..."

"Bishop Murphy didn't go on a mission."

Thank goodness, Allison thought before she could
stop herself from thinking it. "But he wasn't a member of
the church then."

Suddenly the expression on Ashley's face changed and
she looked over at Allison suspiciously. "You don't think I
love Jared either."

"I didn't say that," Allison said. "Brian was my high
school sweetheart, too." Great. Liz was going to kill her.
"I'm just trying to help you see your mother's side of it."

"But she can't take my money, can she?"

There was no way that Allison wanted to answer that
one. Mercifully, the doorbell rang. Allison jumped up to
answer it before she realized it might be Liz and a posse.
She stopped a few feet from the door. "Ashley, does your
mother know where you are?"

"No."

Allison peeped through the peephole just in case. It
was Jared. He was standing awkwardly on the porch with
his hands in his pockets.

"Come on in, Jared," Allison said.

He hesitated. "Is Ashley okay?"

"I think so. Come on in."

He walked over to Ashley and put his hand on her head. "Are you okay?"

She nodded and sniffed.

"Did you tell Sister Lewis about the money?" he asked Ashley. When she nodded he turned to Allison. "Could she really take her money away?"

"Well," Allison said, not wanting to really say anything. "If it has her name on it she probably can. But I really don't think she would do that." She looked back and forth at the two gloomy young people before her. "Do you?"

They both nodded.

Allison looked back at them then glanced down at her watch. Visiting hours were running out. Then she got a great idea. Well, at least part of it was great. One part of it was a little frightening but she could handle it. Maybe.

"Why don't you spend the night here, Ashley? We can talk some more when I come home from the hospital. That will give both you and your mother time to think." That was the easy part of the plan. "I'll call your mother and see if that's okay." That was the frightening part. "Okay?"

"Will you ask her not to take my money?" Ashley asked.

Allison did not feel worthy at all of the faith Ashley seemed to have in her. "Well, we'll see how the conversation goes. Okay?"

Fortunately for Allison that ambiguous answer satisfied Ashley so she left them and went to make the phone call. She decided to let it ring four times and if Liz hadn't answered by that time then Allison would know that she wasn't divinely inspired about the call.

Liz picked up the phone in the middle of the fourth ring.

"Liz," Allison said. "Is it all right if Ashley spends the night over here after she babysits?"

"Will Jared be there?"

"Of course not, Liz," Allison said patiently. Liz had a way of immediately putting Allison right back on Ashley's and Jared's side. "She's just a little upset and I told her maybe you and she both needed some time to think."

Liz didn't answer right away. "Did she say anything about marrying Jared?"

"We've talked a little about her and Jared. She's not going to do anything rash right now. They both are good kids, Liz." Good kids crazy in love. "So can she stay?"

"I guess so. But I want her home tomorrow — without Jared."

"I'll see she gets to school in the morning."

"Okay then," Liz said.

Suddenly Allison felt inspired and unusually courageous. "And, Liz," she said. "You try not to do anything you might regret either." Then the inspiration and courage left her immediately and she hung up the phone before Liz could answer.

22

*W*hen Allison got home from the hospital that night Ashley was fast asleep in Sharon's bed. Sharon said she was exhausted from crying so much. So Allison didn't see her until breakfast the next day.

She came in from taking Melinda out to her minibus to find Ashley lingering over her orange juice. Sharon and Andrew were finishing up getting ready for school so Allison sat down across from her.

"Do you feel like going to school today?" she asked her kindly.

"I guess so," Ashley said. "I don't want to go home."

"What are you going to do when you go home?"

"I don't know. What do you think I should do?"

"That's a good question." Allison thought a minute. She and Brian had discussed the tricky triangle the night before. "Why don't you go home and tell your mother that you aren't going to do anything crazy and that it will really hurt you if she withdraws all your money. She has to be proud of you for saving so much."

"I doubt it."

"Can you talk to your Dad?"

"Yes. But he's out of town until tomorrow."

"Well, why don't you just see if you can be real brave until then. Then I'm sure things will be better." Allison squeezed her hand. "And if you want to and your mother doesn't care you can always stay here tonight after the pizza party." The Young Women had decided to have a pizza party at Allison's house to celebrate Brian's homecoming. "Now you'd better get ready for school or you'll be late."

The first bell was ringing when Allison pulled up in front of the high school to let the girls out after they had missed the bus. Ashley spied Jared waiting for her so she jumped right out of the car, but Sharon stayed behind and looked secretive.

"The bell's ringing, honey."

"I know, Mom. But," Sharon said. She looked out to see where Ashley was, "I thought you would want to know that Ashley said something this morning about eloping."

"What!" Allison practically screamed. "What did she say?"

"When you were out in the car blowing the horn she said that it might be easier to just elope. Then her mother couldn't keep them apart." She kissed Allison on the cheek. "I've got to go. Have a nice day."

Allison watched in a stupor as Sharon got out of the car. She was almost out of earshot when Allison finally came to and slid quickly across the seat to unroll the window. "Sharon, Sharon," she shouted.

"What, Mom?" Sharon looked around to see if anyone had heard her mother screaming.

"Tell Ashley when you see her that we expect her at the pizza party tonight. We expect her."

"Okay." Sharon started walking again.

"Sharon!"

"What, Mom?"

"And tell her to bring some napkins. We've got to have napkins there." The assignment technique always worked for homemaking meeting.

"Okay." Then Sharon started running.

As Allison slid back across the seat Mark asked from the back seat, "What are you going to do today, Mommy?"

She put the car in gear and pulled off. "First, I'm going to take you two to the Y, then I'm going to pick up Daddy, then I might just collapse." And pray that Sharon had terribly misunderstood what Ashley had said.

23

She didn't get to collapse until six o'clock that evening at which time she fell into a chair in the family room. Since she had picked up Brian from the hospital that morning she had spent the rest of her day putting her house back in order. She figured if she would just work fast and furiously for one more mixed-up afternoon that her whole life would be back in order and she could start living normally again. Then maybe she could lock her whole family up in the house with her and keep the problems away until she rested up. It sounded good anyway. And Sharon hadn't called her from school so evidently Ashley hadn't disappeared under mysterious circumstances after all.

The children were thrilled that their Daddy was home and were gathered around him on the couch telling him all at once everything that had happened to them while he had been gone. The scene was peaceful and happy enough to be an Ensign cover.

"I guess I'd better go do something about my appearance," Allison said wearily.

"I don't know why you decided to have a Young Women activity here tonight," Brian said. "You could have postponed it."

"Honey, the only thing I have done so far as Young Women President is have one activity then hide out for two weeks in the hospital, dumping all my children on the Young Women and their mothers."

"So what's happening tonight?" he asked.

"They wanted to have a pizza party so they are bringing everything over to our house. I left it all up to them." Then she sighed. "I certainly hope Ashley shows up. Sharon didn't get to talk to her again during school but she did see her getting on the bus after school."

"Can I come to the pizza party?" Brian asked.

"Only if you behave." She looked over at the children. "Okay, boys, I guess it's time to get your pajamas on."

"Oh no, Mom," Sharon said quickly. "Let them stay in their clothes. Just for a little while."

"Why?" Allison asked. It sounded a little radical to her.

"Well," Sharon fumbled. "They might — might get pizza on their clean pajamas."

"Are you up to something, girl?" Brian asked.

"No," she said innocently. "Just leave them in their clothes and I'll help them change later."

"Something is going on," Brian said.

"I'll never tell," Sharon said mysteriously. Then she fled the room.

Brian looked at Allison with bewilderment. "Did she actually volunteer to help with the boys?"

"Honey, she has really been great," Allison said. "If she wants to have a secret it's all right with me." She reluctantly pulled herself up from her chair. "Can you handle things while I get ready?"

"Sure," Brian said. He turned to Melinda who was sitting beside him in her wheelchair and picked her hands up. "Melinda and I are going to sit here and yell for our pizza. We want pizza, we want pizza."

The boys loved the game and joined in enthusiastically. With everyone adequately occupied, Allison left with a contented feeling in her heart.

Within a half an hour all the Young Women, except Ashley, arrived, pizzas and Seven-ups in hand. As they lined up in the family room and faced Brian and Allison they alternated between giggling and looking secretive.

Brian and Allison looked expectantly at them then looked at each other. Finally Jennifer said, "Well, say something, Terri Lynn. You're the president."

"Surprise!" Terri Lynn said. She handed Brian and Allison each a pizza and they all giggled again.

"Thank you," they both said. Then they waited.

Jennifer rolled her eyes. "We're waiting, Terri Lynn."

"Oh okay," Terri Lynn said. She handed Brian and Allison each a Seven-Up. "We're giving you a date tonight."

"They thought of it, Mom," Sharon said. "They wanted to give you two a date since you've had such a bad time."

"So we're going to take the children out for a hamburger and then to a movie," Erin said. "And you can stay here and eat pizza and listen to music or something. I guess you can't dance yet, Brother Lewis."

Everyone giggled again. Allison didn't know what to think. She thought they would have been tired of babysitting by this time.

"But girls," she said. "You've been so sweet helping with the children that you deserve the party. I haven't done anything for you."

"Oh but you have, Sister Lewis," Terri Lynn said. "And we enjoyed babysitting. Even Jennifer did."

Jennifer didn't say anything until Erin poked her in the back. "Yeh, it was okay," she finally admitted.

"Well, thank you," Allison said. "I don't know what to say."

"Say yes then," Sharon said.

Allison looked back at Brian who shrugged his shoulders in surrender. "I wouldn't mind spending the evening with a good-looking woman," he said. He winked at the girls. "I sort of miss all those nurses." The girls giggled again.

"But can you take care of Melinda?" Allison asked.

"Mom," Sharon said. "We've been taking care of her. She wants to go."

Melinda nodded as vigorously as she could, keeping her eyes on Allison for the decision to be announced.

Allison hesitated only a moment after that. "Oh, okay," she said. "If you're sure you can handle it."

"We're sure," Erin said. "Go get your coats, boys. My parents are waiting in the car."

"I'll push Melinda," Andrew said.

"Call us if you need us, okay?" Allison said. "You have our number?"

"Yes, Mother," Sharon said patiently.

Before Allison could think of any more protests they were out the door and down the ramp singing Matthew's favorite song "Pingle Bells" even though it was only October. She shut the door behind them, checked out the front window, and went back to Brian.

"Bring some ice and glasses, honey, and let's get this party going," he said.

"Ashley didn't come, Brian. Do you think..?" Allison said. Maybe she should call and see where she was.

"Maybe Jared is going to bring her and they're just late."

"I don't know." An ominous feeling clutched her heart.

"Well, why don't you come and eat some pizza before it gets cold. If they aren't here by the time we finish you can call."

Allison hesitated only a minute. After all, Liz hadn't called her so it couldn't be that bad.

Brian was already digging into the pizza as Allison went for the crystal glasses. Maybe this isn't such a bad idea, she thought. She and Brian certainly deserved a little enjoyment after what they'd been through.

24

As Allison walked into the family room with the glasses for their drinks, the phone rang. She hesitated — tempted not to answer it since it couldn't possibly be the children already. But as she debated the doorbell rang, too, so with a frustrated sigh she yelled, "Can you get the phone, Brian — I'll get the door." Maybe it was the paperboy.

It wasn't the paperboy, though. It was two policemen.

"Are you Allison Lewis?" one of them asked. He looked down at a notebook.

"Allison," Brian called. "Liz is on the phone. Something about Ashley and Jared eloping and some policemen coming over to talk to you."

"They're here," Allison said. She invited them in. "I'm not avoiding questioning or anything," she added nervously. "But could I go get this call and see what this is about?" She knew she was entitled to one phone call.

"Sure," the policeman said jovially.

"Come on in and have a piece of pizza," she said. "Do you like pepperoni?" They followed her into the family room. "Honey, this is Detective Mason and Epps," she said, reading from their badges. "This is Brian, my husband. He just had back surgery." She picked up the phone Brian handed her as Detective Mason began to share his history of back problems with Brian.

"Liz, what's wrong?" she asked.

"Ashley and Jared have eloped," Liz said with panic in her voice. "Where are they?"

"I don't know, Liz," Allison said. "I haven't seen her since I dropped her off at school this morning. How do you know they've eloped?"

"She left a note and her suitcase is gone." Liz started crying. "She just has to get married in the temple. She just has to."

Allison had to know. "Liz, did you withdraw her money from the bank?"

"How did you know about that?"

"She told me," Allison said. "So did you?"

"Yes, I did," she said defensively. "I just couldn't let her use it to marry that boy. She can have it back when she goes to college."

"Well, I don't know where she is and I've got to go explain that to two policemen that you sent to my house."

"I told them you would know where she was."

"I don't know where they are, Liz," Allison said, getting very irritated. Just watch. Brian's first night home and she'd spend it in jail, accused of withholding information.

"Please, please, help me," Liz said. "She's so young."

Allison didn't trust herself to say anything else — she just hung up. She went back to the two detectives and told them everything she knew about Ashley and Jared which included no ideas about where they were. Each of the policemen enjoyed a couple of pieces of pizza and a glass of Seven-Up before they stood up and said they had to leave.

"Sure hope your back does okay," Detective Mason said. "Thanks a lot, Mrs. Lewis."

Brian handed Allison a piece of now lukewarm pizza. "So what happened?" he asked.

She explained it to him, then said, "You don't think they'll do anything, do you?"

"I don't know," he said. "But sit over here by me and let's enjoy what's left of our date. We'll worry about Ashley afterward."

She snuggled down beside him, his arm around her. "If the doorbell rings again I'm not answering it."

As soon as the words left her mouth the doorbell rang. Brian said, "So do you want me to get it this time?"

"No, I will. Maybe it's Ashley." She got up reluctantly, taking a big bite of pizza before she left. "Keep my spot and pizza warm."

"Hi, Bishop Murphy," she said thirty seconds later. "Come on in."

"We heard Brian was home and the wife insisted that I bring this over." He handed her two yellow pies. "Well, actually I suggested it. I hate to come over empty-handed."

"Oh bishop, don't ever hesitate to come over empty-handed," she said earnestly. "Not ever. Never."

"Don't worry about it," he said. "It was either bring the pies over or eat them myself, and I can't stand squash."

Join the club, she thought. But she said, "Thank you. I'll take them into the kitchen. You can go see Brian in there." She waved in the direction of the family room.

When she got to the kitchen she put the pies on the table, then remembered the children's rating system and moved them onto the counter to the place of honor closest to the garbage can. Then she got down another glass and filled it with ice for their new guest. Maybe he wouldn't stay long and she and Brian could salvage a half hour together.

The bishop and Brian were deep in a discussion about tax credits and some kind of income that was both adjusted and gross so Allison picked up one of the few remaining pieces of now-cold pizza and sat down in the chair beside the window. Maybe the paperboy would still come. As she looked out she saw a car pull up slowly behind the bishop's. Whoever it was just sat there in the dark.

She sat up, looking closer as it occurred to her that it looked like Jared's car. Then, as both front doors opened and two people got out, she knew it was them. Allison looked over at the bishop and Brian who were still talking seriously about something boring so she decided to handle this herself. If she was going to be arrested for harboring fugitives she would need Brian to be innocent and take care of the children.

They didn't even notice her leave the family room. She walked quietly through the living room and opened the door before they could ring the bell.

"Ashley, Jared," she said. "It is you."

They walked past her as she searched their faces for signs of remorse or sorrow but they looked pretty happy to her. And neither one of them was wearing a wedding ring.

Allison motioned them to be quiet and led them back into the hall. When they got there she faced them and said, "Do you know how worried your mother is, Ashley?"

"She probably called the police," Jared said.

"They were just here," Allison said. "And they ate my pizza."

"Sorry," Jared said.

"Never mind," Allison said. "Where have you been?"

"It's a long story," Ashley said.

"I have a long time," Allison said. "Your mother said you left a note saying you were eloping. Did you?"

"Yes," Ashley said. "I mean I left a note but we didn't elope." She reached for Jared's hand and clasped it tightly. "We started to, but just couldn't."

"Why not?" Allison asked. But that didn't sound thankful enough that they hadn't so she added, "I'm glad you didn't, but why didn't you?"

Ashley started to talk but stopped when tears filled her eyes. Jared looked down at her and put his arm around her. "It was because of you," he said.

"Me?" Allison asked. All she had done this evening was answer the door and eat a little cold pizza.

"We want a marriage like you and Brian have and we know that means going to the temple," Ashley said.

"And a mission," Jared added. Ashley didn't say anything else — she reached out and put her arms around Allison. Allison hugged her back.

"Well," Allison said. "Whatever the reason, you made the right decision. But I knew you would."

She held Ashley back and looked at her. "Now, why don't you two go in the family room and get some pizza. I'll call your mother and tell her you're here."

"Could I stay here tonight?" Ashley asked.

"Sure," Allison said. "Then I'll take you home in the morning and you can have a nice long talk with your mother." There went another night's sleep worrying about that little trip.

This evening is not turning out as I planned, she thought, and I didn't even plan it. But at least it's quiet without the children interrupting every two seconds.

"Honey, we're out of pizza," Brian said.

"You didn't save me a piece?"

"You can have my crusts," the bishop graciously offered.

"No thanks. We have other guests anyway so I'll go see what I have in the freezer and refrigerator."

"Who's here?" Brian asked.

"Jared and Ashley," Allison said triumphantly.

"They didn't elope?" Brian asked.

The bishop looked over at Brian. "Elope?" he said. "As in marry? I'm confused."

Allison wouldn't touch that one with a ten foot pole so she left and let Brian do the explaining.

A few minutes later she had an armful of Jeno pizza rolls, some of which she was going to have, some frozen Twinkies, a box of popsicles, and two Relief Society meat loafs. With the several loaves of homemade bread still on her table and some apple juice it made a feast.

Jared and Ashley were in the family room talking about Youth Conference and Brian was on the phone when she got back in the family room.

"Ashley, your mother said you can stay here tonight," Allison said. "And for some reason she said she has forgiven me. And that you can talk about the bank account."

"That's great," Ashley said.

"Honey," Brian said, covering the phone with his hand. "It's Sharon. She says that Matthew has wet his pants, Mark has thrown up, and Melinda is crying because of a werewolf picture in the lobby of the theater. She wants to know what to do."

Allison threw her hands up in the air and laughed at the impossibility of it all. "Tell them to come home and join the pizza party."

He told her and hung up the phone. "Sharon says she's sorry and thank you and she'll clean up her room tomorrow."

A few minutes later, when Allison had finally filled her plate with pizza rolls, Twinkies, and a meat loaf sandwich, she walked to the door of the family room and surveyed the party. Melinda was content lying beside her daddy, eating a pizza roll. Matthew had fallen asleep in Erin's arms as Mark and Andrew played video games with Jennifer and Jared. The rest of the girls were looking through the albums in hope of finding one they wanted to listen to. The bishop was hopelessly involved in solving a Rubik's Cube.

None of them saw Allison but as she looked at each one of them she thought how each of them had caused her worry and heartache in the past few weeks but had also given her the love and strength to turn it into the happiness she felt now.

Maybe, just maybe, she thought as she popped a cold pizza roll in her mouth. Maybe she could be a rock one day. Or maybe she already was.